STARRY SKIES FOR MY OMEGA

MARIANNA FORREST

❀ Created with Vellum

ACKNOWLEDGMENTS

First off, I want to send out a big thank you to everyone who helped in the making of this book! Ya'll are saints, each and every one of you!

To C.W. Gray: Thank you for introducing me to this genre! Let it be known that you have been a huge inspiration to me since the day we met. Thank you for all your pointers and words of encouragement!

To my editor, Beth: Thank you so much for all your hard work! I've learned a lot from you, and it is a pleasure to work with you!

To Chris: Thank you for your time, tips, and tricks! Without you, my hands would have remained idle, and this Omegaverse world would have never come to fruition. You rock, man!

And finally, a big thank you to, well... you! Yes, you, the reader! You're as much a part of this story as the people listed above! Thank you for picking this book up, and I hope you enjoy it!

Much love,
Marianna Forrest

armth. He felt warmth. Another person nearby, perhaps. He felt light touches across his body, cool against his flesh. Strong arms drew him close, framing his head as a masculine body scattered with tattoos and scars seared against his own skin. Just a little more and–

"–morning, good morning, good morning, Boston!"

An excessively jovial voice on the radio echoed throughout the room, jarring Lukas from his dream. He felt a light sweat covering his body. Sunlight peeked through the slits in the curtains, making the room even warmer than it already felt.

He threw his arm across his eyes and groaned. As he turned off the alarm and tried to move his legs, he realized too late that he had disturbed someone's rest. A disgruntled meow came from the depths of the warm quilt.

"Oh, Miss Mulberry, please forgive your careless butler," Lukas chuckled as he reached out to pet the fuzzy creature hidden beneath the quilt. He heard purrs coming from the darkness near his legs as he stroked his fingers through her soft fur.

Lukas was grateful for the tiny creature that was holding his legs hostage. This little gray and white ball of fluff had been clawing her way into his ice-cold heart over the past five years and had helped him through some rough days.

"Do you remember that day as well as I do, Miss Mulberry? It started out as a rough day for both of us, but by the end of it, everything turned out well. Never in my life did I think I would go job hunting and end up getting adopted by a cat," he laughed.

He felt the bundle of warm fur move up his legs before her adorable, scrunched-up face appeared at the edge of the quilt, staring out at him.

"You were such a tiny, feisty little thing, covered in muck and fleas, defending your turf from anyone who tried to get near. Remember that one guy? You gave him one hell of a scratch, you know. He called you a damn cat and everything, but you weren't no damn cat. You didn't run from me, did you? Not when I came back with that nasty-smelling cat food."

All seemed to be forgiven as Miss Mulberry crawled from underneath the quilt to stretch, rubbing against Lukas' back before hopping onto the windowsill nearby. She beckoned her butler to open the curtains further.

Lukas stood from his bed and stretched before granting her wish, taking a look outside himself. The ivy-covered buildings across the street reminded him of just where he was now.

"It's beautiful, isn't it, Miss Mulberry?" He sadly scratched her chin. "You know, you would have loved it back home. Lots of space and sunshine, and tons of mice in the fields."

Mornings in Boston were much different than mornings back home. Whereas in Boston, he saw buildings outside his bedroom window first thing in the morning, he saw dew-covered fields and colorful sunrises in his little community of Bellcrest. It was one of the many things he missed about living in North Carolina.

Sighing deeply, Lukas stretched his arms high over his head, blowing a stray curl of hair out of his face. He turned away from the window and walked over to his dresser, checking his phone before looking at his reflection in the mirror.

Yeesh. He really needed a haircut. His dark, curly locks were starting to get a bit unruly. Running a hand through his hair, he paused. His skin was beginning to take on a dark caramel tone from his work in his garden, making his green eyes stand out.

"Oh damn, I'm turning into Pa." A small smile tugged at his lips. He turned from the mirror, made his way downstairs into the kitchen, and started a pot of water.

Walking over to the pantry, he braced himself as he picked up a bag of cat food. At the sound of mana falling into her dish, the bundle of fluff came sprinting from the stairwell meowing expectantly before promptly skidding on the tile straight into his legs. *Like clockwork, every morning.*

"Well, Miss Mulberry, let's say hello to our dear friend, Mr. Rogers," he muttered to himself, turning on the TV in the living room. The smiling faces of William Rogers and Cathlene Sanders, heads of the local news station, appeared on the screen, their trademark voices sailing smoothly across the room.

The drone of the news anchors always became white noise to him as he focused on his breakfast. Sports, trade market, world news... always the same news.

He was startled as a sudden *moo* blasted through the living room. He turned, seeing a panning shot of a large farm located in Tennessee. Countryside Cherubs, the headline read. *Oh, my heart.* It was baby-season, alright—calves, ducklings, a couple of foals, and piglets dotted the screen as the farmer showed them off.

A pang of homesickness washed over him. He missed his old farm so much. He missed all those critters, and he longed for the calm countryside he used to see outside his bedroom window. The hardest part was how much he wanted to see his family again. Every day he craved his Ma's cooking or his Pa's stupid jokes, maybe even his older brother's teasing.

He jumped as he felt Miss Mulberry rub against his leg, begging for some of the ham he had sitting out to fry. Of course, he would have to give her a piece. After all, he knew he was at her mercy at night after he fell asleep. He felt a smile tugging at his lips. At the very least, he wasn't alone in Boston.

His thoughts drifted to his schedule for the week. Aside from work, he had to get fertilizer for his plants, cat food, and snacks, and he had to be sure to send some flowers to his neighbors, Andre and Dahlia.

Lukas sighed, tapping his pen slowly on the notebook. It had been a few days since he heard Andre's old car roll down the road. Since Dahlia's surgery, he had refused to leave her side to come home even for a minute. It was an unbearable silence, a reminder that some of his favorite people needed a bit of that famed Southern Hospitality right about now.

"Yeah, maybe make some meals, so Andre doesn't have to worry about cooking for a few days while Dahlia recovers," he mumbled to himself.

He scooped the poached eggs and ham onto a

plate and sat at the table to look at his planner. *And I'll have to stop by that quick stop shop and pick up some more bottles of scent blocker.*

The smooth voice of the weather anchor rattled Lukas from his thoughts, letting the fine city of Boston know another perfect sunny week was on the way. He smiled, thankful for the clear weather for the next few days. He would have plenty of time to fix up his garden now.

Finishing his breakfast, he put away his dishes and stretched. *I'll take my tea in the garden, good sir. Mm-yes. Thank you.* He snickered.

Lukas shuffled his way upstairs, a glass of iced tea gripped carefully in his hand. He grabbed a small bucket from the nearby broom closet, his own little toolbox, full of everything you need to be a successful home gardener.

Pushing open the door to the roof, he stepped out into the early-morning sun, letting the cool morning breeze flow across his face and shoulders.

As he rested his elbows on the railing and sipped his tea, his gaze drifted down the street. When he'd first moved to Boston, he definitely hadn't done his research. All he knew was that his Ma had once owned an old townhouse in the area. Honestly, he had expected tall buildings and parking lots without a hint of green within the city limits. Imagine his surprise when he found out the Boston Public Gardens were right down the street from his home! *I'll have to set up a get-together with Eliseo and Sawyer soon. Maybe a picnic or something once it warms up a bit more.*

Lukas chuckled as he remembered how quickly he had become friends with Eliseo and Sawyer. All it took was some good food, and he had them in the palm of his hand. *Seems to be a running trend, now that I think about it.*

Eliseo was a bit easier to get to know. As an outgoing fashion designer, Eliseo was always talking, laughing, and smiling. He often carried around a sketchbook, ready to jot down any notes for his future patterns and designs.

Sawyer, on the other hand, was a bit harder to read. He was quiet and thoughtful, never really saying much until he got to know Lukas. He owned a flower shop and often preferred to enjoy the calmer moments of city life, wherever they could be found.

Lukas let out a weary sigh and scanned the streets below. As he stared at the blossoming flowers and vivid green trees down the street, he felt his eyes slowly becoming unfocused. He ran his fingers across the iron railing, trying to block out the sounds of the city to home in on the birds nearby. All that was missing was the scent of the morning dew and the livestock, and he would almost believe he was back home.

The sound of a neighbor slamming their car door snapped him back to reality, and he was once again on his roof, staring out at the shimmering waters of the Charles River. Sighing, he sat on his nearby wicker bench. More people were waking up now, eager to start their days.

He had heard city people never adhered to any schedule, believed that their days were always different. Still, time and time again, he saw the same people pass by his home each morning, each with the same routine. People really were creatures of habit, even surrounded by an ever-moving concrete jungle.

Spotting Ms. Karson leaving her home, he realized just how late it was getting. He quickly sipped the last of his tea, checking hurriedly on his plants before rushing back down the stairs. He heard a clamor in the bedroom, a telltale sign that Miss Mulberry was about to get into some trouble.

Lukas rounded the corner just in time to see Miss Mulberry miss the jump to the windowsill from his dresser, slipping with the grace of a free-falling elephant right into a basket of clean clothes. He barely held back a laugh when she looked around and settled down in the basket as if she had meant to fall into it.

"And thus, the weekly Christening of Fur has been completed. Thank you, Miss Mulberry," he smiled as he herded her out of the basket. He heard his phone go off on the dresser, his boss asking him to grab a coffee from Rufio on his way to work. That could only mean one thing.

"It's gonna be crazy when I get there. He must be running behind this morning," Lukas groaned.

His boss might own the best diner this side of Boston, but even the top dog himself had to admit that Rufio's coffee cart sold the best in Boston. Lukas personally didn't enjoy coffee, but he had heard the word around town.

But first, shower.

He dug to the bottom of the hamper to avoid the fur-covered clothing. He picked out a faded plaid shirt, jeans, and a clean apron before stepping into the bathroom to get ready for work.

As he stood under the warm stream of water, he thought back to his dream. He typically only had that type of dream when his heat was close. Usually, he kept a strict detail concerning it and checked it multiple times throughout the months leading to his heat. Had he lost track of the days? He seriously couldn't forget that blocker.

"Mmm. Damn if it wasn't a good dream, though,"

he mumbled to himself, sighing as the steam rose around his body.

He stepped out of the shower and pulled on his fresh clothing before throwing his apron over his shoulder.

Even though he was a bit early, he could already hear the angry drivers on the roads nearby. Since moving to Boston, traffic had become his worst nightmare. He quickly became thankful for public transportation, blessing the bus drivers for putting up with the demons of the highway.

"Well, Miss Mulberry, I'm off. I'm trusting you to watch the house."

A trill came from the windowsill where the little bundle of fluff was birdwatching.

Lukas grabbed his old ball cap before he stepped outside, locking the door behind him. It was late April in Boston. The warmth of the morning sun slowly drew people from their homes. Joggers bounded down the sidewalk, passing behind the benches spotted with people enjoying their coffee and chattering about their upcoming summer vacations.

While it didn't seem to bother anybody else, the city smog started to make Lukas' eyes water. Yet another thing he would never get used to. Wiping his eyes, he spotted Rufio down the road selling coffee to some teenagers.

Rufio spotted him coming and waved as the teenagers walked off. His good mood was always infectious, and his customers always left with smiles on their faces.

Lukas grinned and waved back, picking up his pace so he could spend a few minutes talking to Rufio before a bus arrived.

Nearing the cart, he heard Rufio call out, "Oi,

Lukas, great to see ya this fine morning! Will it be the usual?"

"Actually, the boss wants to try something a bit different. He leaves the choice in your capable hands," Lukas replied, enjoying the smell of the roasting coffee beans.

Rufio grinned slyly, rubbing his hands together.

"Hmm, I have just the thing. Watch me work my magic," he said in a dark tone as he sank behind the cart.

Rufio reappeared with an armful of fresh ingredients and bottles. With a flick of his wrist and the clank of the bottles, Rufio began working at a speed that flawlessly showcased his years of experience in the barista business.

Within a few minutes, he presented a rather normal-looking cup of coffee to Lukas. Noting the look of confusion on Lukas' face, Rufio grinned and explained himself.

"Now that, my friend, is a cup of mint-infused iced coffee. All it takes is a bit of love, and some of that there minty-fresh goodness, and you have yourself a coffee that will get you through any shite-storm this city may throw at you. It'll shock the boss-man awake, that's for damn sure."

Rufio crossed his arms and closed his eyes before giving Lukas a curt nod.

Warily, Rufio's eyes opened slightly, looking around for anyone within earshot before saying, "I wouldn't have ever thought about selling something like this in my stall, but I heard it was getting pretty popular. Or so the hipsters I hear nowadays say. I used my legendary stealth skills to steal the recipe from them," he grinned.

Lukas wrinkled his nose as a strong scent of mint hit him, "I wonder if Eliseo would like this."

"Lukas, that boy loves anything coffee. You don't have to worry about him. Now me, I would never drink that swill. I'll just stick with my usual black coffee. Though sometimes, if I'm feeling really good like I am this morning, I put a little bit of my good whiskey in it."

A wide smile crossed his face as he tapped a flask hanging from his hip.

"My old friend here has been with me through thick and thin. Mostly thick, though. Yessir, thick. I mean, just look at me. Obviously, I ain't one to shy away from my wife's cooking."

Rufio softly patted his belly before a wheezy laugh burst from his timeworn body.

The sight of the bus coming down the road ended their brief conversation. Lukas quickly thanked Rufio for his time and coffee and passed some bills to the vendor.

"Now, wait just a minute, Lukas. Take this too." Rufio ducked behind the cart and pulled out a small container.

Lukas took the container carefully, eyeing the contents, half expecting something to jump out at him. "Please don't be a spider."

Rufio crossed his arms, grumbling. "Hurtin' my feelings over here."

He was pleasantly surprised by the sight of a baked good tucked safely inside the sealed bowl.

"Cake? Did you put whiskey in this, too?" he asked the vendor with a smile.

"Nah. I only got so much to spare. It's just a little extra gift for you and the boss-man to split. Because ya'll put up with me so much," Rufio replied with a toothy grin.

Lukas hastily tried to dig more money out of his

wallet, almost dropping his apron before Rufio stopped him.

"I said it's a gift, boy. A gift is free, don't ya know? Now go on, you're gonna miss your ride!"

Lukas quickly thanked the vendor before sprinting to the bus stop. He barely caught the attention of the driver before she pulled away from the curb.

He heard a distant reply as he stepped onto the bus. He gripped the bowl tightly before slumping against a pole near the front of the bus. He felt people staring at his back, silently questioning his breathlessness.

The bus jerked forward, garnering groans of disapproval from the passengers. He felt the stares taper off as people returned to their business.

Lukas sighed before whispering to himself, "And now, time to actually start the day."

elcome to the Roaring Ridgemont Eatery: a hole in the wall, lost down the hidden path, retro diner of Boston. Located absolutely nowhere near Ridgemont, the place was a favorite meeting and eating spot of young, old, and all in between.

Why did he even name this place after Ridgemont when it's miles away? Lukas wiped down a recently emptied table. He sighed, listening to the clanks, clinks, and clangs of the diner that drowned out the cheery tune playing over the speakers.

"Lukas, Mr. Jenkins' order is ready! He's sitting out on the patio today! And when you get a chance, Ms. Newman needs some extra creamer for her coffee!" came a booming voice from the kitchen.

That booming voice had a name: Archer Moody, the head-honcho. Also known as the man who would probably go down in history for being the swiftest path to a heart attack. He didn't almost just jump out of his skin. No siree.

Pushing the pointless thoughts from his mind, he slapped a smile on his face as he spun around to pick up the order. "Sure thing, Boss!"

"And Mrs. Xian needs some wipes for Yijun!" the voice from the kitchen frantically added.

Lukas wondered why the man was so distraught but then he caught sight of the toddler covered in pancake syrup as Mrs. Xian tried to clean him up. How did such a small child manage to squeeze the entire bottle all over the table and floor? Such strength and persistence!

It had been crazy from the moment he stepped into the diner. His boss was such a mess that he was surprised the diner hadn't been engulfed in flames before opening time. Despite not opening for another fifteen minutes, people had still gathered outside in numbers. He felt the eyes of the expectant people on his back as he rolled silverware and set out menus before unlocking the doors. No wonder his boss had wanted to pay a bit extra for Rufio's coffee today.

Heading back to the front, Lukas ducked behind the counter to gather everything he needed, dodging the frenzied movements of his boss. He reached for the tray after loading it down, but his boss stopped him before he could rush off.

"Wait, Lukas. Here." Archer scooped another spoonful of fresh berries over the Danish Mr. Jenkins ordered.

Lukas was a bit confused but rushed off to Mr. Jenkins. As he stepped out onto the patio, he was increasingly thankful for his old ball cap. The sun was still low enough that it was peeking under the awning set up on the patio, and it was a brutal ball of blazing death despite it being so early in the morning.

Seeing the old man, he realized exactly why his boss had put extra goodies on the plate at the last minute. The ordinarily chatty old man looked like he'd had a rough morning.

Dressed in a fine vest with suspenders and slacks, Mr. Jenkins adjusted his glasses, his nose buried in a book. On the other side of the table, a fresh tulip lay next to an old black and white photo of a happy couple that had been framed with care.

Lukas felt his eyes burn for a moment before blinking back the feeling. The picture was of Mr. Jenkins and his wife Nora at their wedding. Had it really been that long since…? Swallowing the lump in his throat, he stepped closer to the table with a smile.

"Hey, Mr. Jenkins, got your usual hot and ready." Lukas carefully put down a plate, heavy with a fresh berry and cream cheese Danish before following it with a cup of hot coffee.

"Ah, wonderful. That's just the way I like it." Mr. Jenkins put the small book he was reading off to the side, looked up, and smiled.

Oh great, now that song is gonna be stuck in my head all day.

"Now, son, I think there's a bit extra here. I don't think I'll be able to finish it all."

"Don't you worry about it, Mr. Jenkins. Yes, there is a bit of extra this time. Archer threw another helping of berries on there for you. If you don't finish it, I can put together a little box for you," Lukas replied, placing the hot cup of coffee on the table.

"You lot are too good to an arthritic old fart like me." He laughed hoarsely. "That's what she always used to call me whenever she was in a jabbing mood."

A peaceful silence filled the patio area as Lukas smiled. "It's a beautiful picture. She looks very happy.

Mr. Jenkins looked down at his plate. "It's been a year today."

The old man gazed at the photo for a short while.

"You know, she was the most beautiful, kindest woman I ever had the pleasure of knowing. I would have been content just being near her, but then I got to marry her. She chose me. Out of all the fools she could have had, she chose me."

A sad smile formed on his face before he said in a hoarse voice, "I hope you don't mind an old man taking up space in your diner today. It's just nice being able to get out of that empty house and be surrounded by friendly faces."

"Mr. Jenkins, if you ever need any company, please stop by here. We're always happy to see you." A sympathetic smile crossed Lukas' face.

"Thank you, son. That means a lot to me. Now go on. You have other people to take care of, too," Mr. Jenkins whispered, patting Lukas on the arm.

Making his way back inside, Lukas tugged his ball cap further down over his eyes. He wasn't going to cry at work, damn it. Archer would worry himself to death.

Before he got very far, a sing-song voice echoed from across the diner, "Is that my Lukas I see?"

He flinched, just a little bit, before turning in the direction of the shrill voice. You could always tell when Ms. Newman was in the room. She was a sweet middle-aged woman with a big heart and a big voice who loved to play matchmaker. Her heart was always in the right place, bless her, but her matches never seemed to stick together long.

"'tis I, Ms. Newman! I heard a tale on the wind that you need a few extra creamers, and I have come to deliver," Lukas nodded.

Ms. Newman let out a hearty laugh before replying, "My, my, Lukas, you act like you're right out of a storybook with those uppity, fancy phrases. Now tell me, how did that date go? I've been sitting on the edge of my seat since last week! He seemed like such a nice young man."

Lukas winced at the reminder of the date.

"Well, he was very kind, and I'm sure he'll make someone very happy someday, but something just didn't click for us." Lukas resisted adding that his date had his eyes on a beta sitting at the table next to them the entire time.

The cheerful lady looked a little down at first before perking back up and saying, "Don't worry, Lukas. He was a beta, and they're a whole different ball game. A bit of hit or miss, and definitely not for everybody. I can set you up with a nice alpha if you give me a few days."

"While I appreciate the offer, Ms. Newman, call me crazy, but I just get this gnawing feeling that something big is just around the corner, and I need to be ready for it," Lukas replied. He gave her a slight smile before setting her extra creamer on the table. No sense in hurting her feelings, after all.

"Oh, that's okay, sweetie, I understand. But you have to promise me that if you meet someone you like, you'll introduce me to them," Ms. Newman replied with a smile.

"I promise. Now, I have to hop back to it. Please enjoy your breakfast," he replied with a smile before rushing off to his last table.

In the time it had taken to drop off Mr. Jenkins' food and Ms. Newman's creamers, he had forgotten just how bad it was at Mrs. Xian's table.

Keeping a brisk pace, he headed over to the syrup-covered table, determined to put a stop to the scene before the toddler somehow managed to find some feathers to roll in. He was pretty sure he'd seen a half-finished chicken costume somewhere in the breakroom not too long ago. Why? Well, Archer was his boss, after all, but honestly, he had no idea. He just didn't feel like tempting fate today.

"Here you go, Mrs. Xian. I saw that Yijun was in a bit of a sticky situation." He grinned. He stealthily confiscated the empty syrup bottle and handed some wipes to the woman.

Mrs. Xian laughed, slowly shaking her head before taking the wipes gratefully.

"I am so sorry for the mess, Lukas. With my wife out of town for work, I've been a bit distracted trying to juggle my own work and being a mom." She smiled, balancing her toddler on her leg while working on her laptop.

How she had managed to keep Yijun from getting any syrup on the laptop was beyond him. Must be a mom thing.

"It's no problem, Mrs. Xian. Just let me know if you need anything else."

The woman sighed, quickly disguising her fatigue with a smile.

"I just need a live-in nanny for the next two weeks until Liu is back. I miss her so much. Our poor little ones have so much energy, and they want to show me everything they've done at school, and I just can't keep up with them."

"Well, I know sugar is the last thing you want for your kids, but if you ever need a little pick-me-up, I can make you a couple of those pineapple buns you like," Lukas offered.

Mrs. Xian's eyes lit up, "That would be wonderful, Lukas, but if it's too much trouble, please don't worry about it."

"It's no trouble at all. I'll have them for you, say, this coming Thursday." Lukas offered a couple more wipes and refilled her coffee.

"Sounds like a plan, Lukas. Thank you so much.

Can you say 'thank you,' Yijun? Say, 'thank you.'" Mrs. Xian bounced Yijun on her leg. The toddler was a giggling mess, trying to speak but mostly babbling, raising his arms up toward Lukas.

Lukas laughed as Mrs. Xian passed Yijun to him. There were only a few people in the diner now, so he could afford to hold a cute toddler for a few minutes.

Yijun was happy as a clam being held so high above the table. Lukas began bouncing him around on his hip and dancing with him in the middle of the diner, much to the toddler's delight. Lukas could see Ms. Newman in the corner booth with a dreamy smile on her face.

He heard his boss call out that another order was ready. He passed Yijun back to his mother and began walking back to the counter.

After he dropped off the order, he returned to ask Mrs. Xian, "By the way, where are Mei and—"

He didn't have time to finish his thought before a little girl of about nine darted from under the table and tackled him with a hug.

Unable to withstand the sudden force of the child, he fell backward onto the floor, catching her before she rolled off him. A little boy of about five jumped into the pile, laughing as Lukas played dead.

Suddenly, the diner filled with a furious vibe. Lukas propped himself up on his elbows and looked toward Mrs. Xian and he wouldn't have been surprised if she had the fires of hell behind her.

A thunderous voice came from the small woman sitting at the table. "Mei, Jin! You have until the count of three to sit at this table and behave or so help me—"

The children scampered back to the table, and their mother returned to her usual, sunny self.

"When I say you stay at this table, I mean it," Mrs.

Xian continued, scolding her normally well-behaved children.

"Anyway, Lukas, thank you for the offer of those pineapple buns. We're going to head out to the park now. Lord knows, these three have enough energy to burn." Mrs. Xian sighed before gathering her children and preparing to leave.

Mei and Jin were already jumping up and down again before their mother glared at them.

"We're getting more pineapple buns!?" the children squealed.

"Yes, Mr. Lukas was nice enough to offer to bake some more for us on Thursday. Now, what do we say?" Mrs. Xian asked them.

"Thank you, Mr. Lukas," Mei and Jin said in unison. Yijun babbled, reaching his hands toward Lukas with a giggle. Lukas ruffled his hand through the toddler's hair.

Mei and Jin hugged Lukas one last time before they followed their mother out of the diner, excited that they were getting their favorite treat soon.

Eventually, the traffic in the diner came to a grinding halt, a welcome change as Lukas sat down on a barstool to catch his breath. The last customers were packing up, ready to head out and face the day. Archer came from the kitchen, wiping his hands on a towel. He tucked a strand of blond hair behind his ear before leaning over the counter to rest.

"Didn't get a chance to thank you for that coffee earlier. I don't think I would have made it without your gracious contribution, Oh Mighty McGuire." He lightly jabbed Lukas on the arm.

"Don't worry about it. Though I thought for sure you were going to vault the counter and strangle that guy that gave you hell over the temperature of his coffee," Lukas joked.

"I thought about it, but whatever would you do without me if I went to prison?" Archer quipped playfully.

A moment of silence came between the two men as they relaxed after the rush of people. Lukas's fingers idly played with a nearby saltshaker as the last customers left the diner.

"So what is this upcoming fair I heard Mrs. Henley talking about? It seems to have put a lot of people in a good mood," Lukas remarked as he idly watched the traffic pass by outside the diner.

"You mean to tell me you don't know about the Heated Hullabaloo?"

Lukas was taken aback by the shock in Archer's tone. He smiled sheepishly. "I used to work night shifts before you hired me on here, remember? Didn't tend to pay attention to many events going on since I had to sleep during the day."

He had been working here for a little under a year. It was tough in the beginning, what with shifting from night shifts to morning and midday shifts, but he had survived.

Archer still looked as shocked as he had before. "How have you not even heard of it, though? Our seasonal fairs are such a big deal! Why, the food, alone, is to die for. My band is lined up to play a few songs, too."

All at once, the words began to tumble out of Archer's mouth. He went into a trance, talking about his favorite dishes and rides at the fair.

"You know Sheldon Yorke, the owner of the Shattered Gate Bar just down the road? I usually set up a joint booth with him every festival to showcase our food and drink. Only thing is, we may need more help to fill the booth this year."

Lukas' gaze snapped up, "More help? What

happened to his other help? Didn't he use to have like five waiters?"

"You remember Johnathon? I know he and his alpha just had a baby recently, but most of 'em just up and quit. Didn't like the hours, they said. Too late in the evening, they said," Archer replied angrily. "Why the hell did they even apply to a bar if they didn't like being out past eight?"

Archer pinched the bridge of his nose with a huff before continuing, "Anyway, he's hired at least one new waiter that I know of, a dependable boy Sheldon and I know well. He and Sheldon are both good at what they do, but if you want to join the fair team, we may have to help out a bit more than usual this year. I'm sure old Yorke would love to add some of your recipes to the menu."

Lukas felt his face get warm from the praise.

"I'll look into it. My garden is doing well, and I may have some fresh berries in time for the fair. I could do some baked goods, maybe make some more savory dishes." He absent-mindedly began thinking about what recipes he could make.

"Oh, wonderful! It'll be crazy since we're all so short-handed, but just think about all that food," Archer replied with a sparkle in his eyes.

"Hey, Boss, I think you have a bit of drool running down your chin," Lukas pointed out with a laugh.

Archer didn't have time to reply before the next wave of customers started to roll in for brunch.

"Ready yourself, Lukas, they come!" Archer laughed as he strolled back into position by the stoves.

CHAPTER 3

Two weeks passed in a blur. *This fair really has people riled up.* As Lukas sat on a couch jammed in the corner of Archer's office, he struggled to pore over the plans and maps for the fair. It had become harder and harder to focus on his work since Archer had started going to the Shattered Gate Bar to help coordinate the fair.

Someone had to take care of the place while Archer was gone, and the diner was still as busy as before, if not busier. With the added work, Lukas was a bit drained, to say the least, though Archer definitely had it worse. The man was probably surviving only by the saving grace of coffee at this point.

Whenever Archer returned from a trip to the bar, he carried a new scent on him, one of burning wood, spices, and pine. It reminded Lukas a lot of home. It was comforting but at the same time, extremely distracting. The heat that sparked in his chest and abdomen whenever he took a breath was maddening, to say the least.

Lukas jumped as the breakroom door slammed. A chill crept across his skin as Archer stepped into the office carrying a stack of papers, the mysterious scent drifting across the room.

"Hey, Lukas, thanks for coming back to help with the planning. Sienna would have stayed, but little Hazel is sick, and I didn't want to keep her away from her kiddo any longer than I have to." Archer sighed, looking over the planner for the upcoming month.

Taking a deep breath, Lukas willed his nerves to calm before he spoke.

"It's no problem. I'm sure Miss Mulberry can be trusted not to throw any wild parties while I'm gone," Lukas quipped, smiling.

"I don't know, the stories you've told me about that cat say otherwise." Archer laughed. "Anyway, planning this fair is going to be a lot of work, but Mr. Yorke did manage to hire some more help in addition to the fella that already has experience, so hopefully it should be smooth sailing 'til the fair."

"Good. Maybe you'll be able to take a bit of a break. I think your blood is about eighty percent coffee right now." Lukas leaned over the desk to sneak a peek at the planner.

"'tis a mighty brew that runs through my veins. I think I need to offer a worthy sacrifice to Rufio for making such long evenings possible…" Archer's voice trailed off.

Lukas took a step back, hands up, "Whoa, Boss, don't look at me like that. How would you ever survive without my pies and Miss Mulberry stories?"

Archer got a dreamy look in his tired eyes. "Throw me some of those famous fruit tarts, and you'll be just fine."

IT WAS CLOSE TO MIDNIGHT WHEN AN OUTLINE AND

supply list for the fair were finally ready to be sent to Mr. Yorke.

"Oh, the sweet gods of sleep reach out to me." Lukas yawned, stretching his arms over his head. He knew he should have napped before he came back in to help with the fair planning.

"No sleeping yet. We have to get this to Mr. Yorke so he can get started on it right away." Archer stood from his desk, patting Lukas on the back a few times to wake him up. "I just have a few more things I need to do here, and then we can head out."

"Isn't your house in the other direction? Don't worry about it, I'll drop the plans off with Mr. Yorke and then catch the bus from the bar," Lukas replied. "I can meet the new help, too. Give my professional opinion."

Archer put one hand on his desk and turned to face Lukas. "Lukas, I know you grew up in a small town, but surely you know things are very different here in the big city? It is much more dangerous at night for everyone, especially someone like you. Especially now."

Lukas stretched, thinking for a moment. "I think I'll be okay. It's just a short trip, and I'll be sure not to investigate any seedy alleyways or talk to strangers."

"Trust me, I really don't think we should risk that, Lukas," Archer murmured, turning his back to him.

Conversation over, his body language screamed. Lukas bristled with irritation at the fact that he was brushed off so easily. Archer stacked his papers and put away office supplies before pausing, holding up an envelope that had gotten buried between the documents.

"Oh, by the way, that customer left this for you. Again," Archer handed over the small envelope with Lukas' name on it.

"Another one? He's kind of starting to freak me out," Lukas murmured.

Archer nodded. "I see him hanging around this area a lot. Still haven't been able to stall him enough to keep him around until you get back to the counter."

Sighing, Lukas buried his face in his hands. "You know, it wouldn't be so bad if he didn't act so shifty. Always wears that hoodie, never looks up from the ground."

Archer appeared lost in thought before saying, "He uses a scent blocker too. I hate to suggest it, but he may be an abused omega. Probably just looking for friends since he seems most comfortable around you. My guess is he escaped from his controlling alpha. Doesn't happen often, but maybe he got lucky. Or maybe he's just hiding from an alpha he doesn't like."

Archer sat down at his desk. He was quiet for a second. "Though, like you said, it is strange. Just keep an eye on him."

Lukas nodded before stretching his arms above his head and flopping onto the nearby couch.

Archer yawned. "I know you're worn out, so don't worry about coming in tomorrow. I'll open the diner late, and then Sienna and I can handle the dinner rush."

"You should take the whole day off, too. You've worked harder than I have the past few weeks, and Sienna would probably appreciate being able to stay home with Hazel," Lukas said, worried.

Archer thought for a moment and sighed, "Maybe you're right, I won't argue with that. It would be nice to have a mental health day. I'll post notices on the front door and our website before I leave tonight. Ah, the perks of not being part of a corporate chain."

Lukas breathed a sigh of relief and pulled out his phone. "I'll call Sienna and let her know since she should still be up and about. Don't worry about it."

A few minutes passed as Lukas and Sienna chatted over the phone. Archer leaned over his desk and took a deep breath, releasing a sigh as Lukas ended the call.

"Thank you. Now, Lukas, I need to talk with you about one last thing." Archer's tone suddenly turned serious. "I'm sure you don't need me to remind you, but I'm going to anyway. You need to reapply your scent blocker before we head out. Don't take this the wrong way, but I can tell it's about time. We don't want to attract any unnecessary attention."

Lukas tensed up. "I was afraid you might mention that. I know it's coming, and I was going to go to the quick stop shop near my house to get some more blocker."

"Lukas, bear with me here, but this one seems different, so scent blockers may not protect you for long. There are just so many people here, so many alphas. You can't be too careful." Archer looked outside into the darkness of the streets.

"Did you forget you're an alpha, too, Boss?" Lukas asked with a frown.

Archer leaned back in his chair and looked at Lukas before crossing his arms and sighing. The look on his face said he knew Lukas' temper was flaring.

"What I'm saying is that not every alpha has a good moral compass, Lukas. You should stay home as much as possible once this heat hits."

A moment of silence came between the two men. Archer sighed and asked, "Do you have any scent blocker on hand?"

"Yeah, in my locker. It's enough to last me for a

couple of days," Lukas replied nervously, walking to his locker in the breakroom and pulling it open.

Archer let out a little *tsk*. "Alright. Give me a few minutes, and we'll head out. I need to put a few things away and lock up."

"Okay," Lukas replied as he sprayed the scent blocker all over himself, feeling it settle onto his skin with a shudder. He dragged himself out of the breakroom, pulling the door shut behind him. He wandered into the main area of the diner.

The minutes passed too slowly as he waited for his boss. He looked out into the streets, watching the people that walked by the windows of the diner.

He may have seemed calm on the outside, but he was seething on the inside. Why was Archer suddenly treating him like a child? And what did he mean 'this one seems different'? His heats had been the same for years. Consistent, every three months, and they had never once hindered his everyday life or posed a danger to him.

The longer he sat, the more irritated he got, so Lukas stood, grabbing his apron and phone. He knew his own body better than anyone, that much was for sure. He wasn't going to stay here and be treated like a damsel in distress. He carefully snuck out of the diner, locking the door behind him.

Standing outside the diner, he took a deep breath before inspecting the area around the restaurant. The number of people who were out and about this late at night still staggered him. Back home, the streets were nearly empty by this time.

He looked up to the sky, disappointed once again when he didn't see any stars.

"These people don't know what they're missing," he whispered to himself.

As he began walking down the street to the

Shattered Gate Bar, he felt himself growing nostalgic. He used to love watching the stars, but since he had moved to Boston five years ago, he hadn't seen any sign of the twinkling lights at night.

Dodging the scattered people on the sidewalk, he glanced over the fair plans. It seemed like a good lineup. Lots of bands, good food, fireworks, and countless ways to keep cool, just what you'd expect from a fair celebrating the beginning of summer.

He might have loved working in his garden, but he still favored winter over every other season. He remembered when he and his older brother had snuck outside one winter evening, just a couple days before Christmas. Something about finding weird tracks in the snow.

A fresh blanket of snow covered the ground, silencing the already quiet countryside. The breeze was cold, making him all the more appreciative of his warm coat and homemade scarf.

He had thought the world beautiful already and then his brother told him to look at the sky. He remembered gasping at the sight. A full moon lit up the snowfields surrounding them, and thousands upon thousands of twinkling stars filled the dark sky.

He could see the city of Greensboro off in the distance to the southwest, Christmas lights glimmering against the buildings. He collapsed into the snow, eyes still on the sky as his brother joined him. They stayed out in the snow as long as they could, just admiring the stars.

By the time they went back into the house, their ma had noticed they were gone and had given them quite the scolding. Though no matter how angry she was with them for sneaking out in the middle of the night, she still had hot chocolate and dryer-fresh blankets waiting for them.

He might have gotten in trouble, but it was still one of his fondest memories.

He was torn from his thoughts by a sudden noise in the alley he had just passed. He spun around, ready to face whatever monster was about to claw its way out of the alley, only to come face-to-face with a stray dog, its golden fur covered in grime.

"Hey, buddy, what are you doing making all that noise?" he asked before squatting down to pet the dog.

The dog was hopping around like a jackrabbit, tail wagging rapidly, at the sound of a friendly voice. It started sniffing around Lukas' pocket.

"Oh, you probably smell that jerky from dinner. Here, take it," Lukas offered the jerky to the dog, who ate it happily.

"Gotta get going, buddy. I can't stay out here long," Lukas whispered to the dog, giving it one last pat on the head.

He had taken a few steps down the sidewalk when he heard the *tap tap tap* of the dog's nails on the concrete.

"Oh, you're my best friend now, huh? Fair enough." Lukas smiled down at the dog.

"You know, I used to have a dog back home years ago. He was a Shepherd mix, a bit bigger than you are. That dog and I used to get into so much trouble," Lukas said to the dog, reminiscing about his old friend.

They had gone a few blocks when Lukas suddenly felt uneasy. The dog sensed it too, stopping next to him. Amid the people on the sidewalk, Lukas could feel eyes on him, and his gut told him it wasn't a good kind of appreciation. He walked a bit faster, determined to get to the bar as quickly as possible.

He made it past a few shops before gathering the

courage to look behind him. A shadow was tailing him, slowly gaining ground.

"Oh shi–" he gasped as he began to run.

The dog kept up with him, herding him closer to the light of the streetlights. The people scattered on the sidewalk dodged him, trying to avoid whatever commotion was heading their way. He was close to the bar now, just a little farther–

The dog suddenly barked and then Lukas was on the ground, being dragged into a nearby alley. He lay on his stomach, gasping for air, wondering what the hell had just happened to him. He raised his head and saw men's boots.

"What the hell? How did–" Lukas murmured.

He didn't have time to register much before the figure grabbed his arm and hauled him to his feet. This close to his attacker, he got a slightly bitter scent. Alpha. An ice-cold fear jolted through his body. *No, no, no. Not gonna sit back and take this–*

Before he could even finish his thought, the dog was biting the leg of the assailant. Lukas took the opportunity to bite the figure's hand that had been carelessly put in front of his face.

The figure threw Lukas to the ground in a panic. Lukas jolted as his head hit the brick wall behind him, his hat toppling into the darkness of the alley. He slumped to the ground, his hands rushing up to hold his head.

Lukas' world was spinning, but his hand had already found its way around the neck of a glass bottle. He grasped it and smashed it against the wall, swiping out at the man as he got close. A red stream flowed down the attacker's arm.

The man groaned, ignoring his bleeding arm while slowly stalking toward the injured omega. Lukas cringed as warm drops of blood hit his face.

The sound of thundering footsteps brought the fight to a stop, the attacker whirling around to face an unknown opponent.

Lukas caught a flash of red throwing the assailant to the ground. He heard people shouting, but couldn't make out what was being said.

The dog stood protectively in front of Lukas, growling at the stranger. In a flash, the incapacitated man stood and ran, and a couple of people chased after him.

It was over. Lukas knew he was bruised and bleeding. That was definitely gonna smart in the morning. His hand found his old hat and clutched it, and he pulled up his arm to rest it languidly on his knee.

His nose twitched as the stranger stepped closer. Another alpha. Just his luck.

"Stay back. Stay away from me," he tried to growl at the stranger, sounding much less threatening than he had planned. He scooted to the side, trying to get away from the man, cringing as his shoulder hit a solid pile of stacked crates.

"I won't hurt you. I just want to get you out of all this garbage and glass," the stranger said in a husky voice. "Please let me help you."

Lukas winced as pain shot through his legs. If he decided to run, he wouldn't get far on his own.

"Fine. Okay."

Lukas took a deep breath before he felt himself being gently pulled up. He didn't sense any hostility from this alpha. He took in more of the man's scent, a heady, intoxicating blend of pine, spices, and...Wait.

He froze at the exact time he heard the alpha take a deep breath. He looked up and saw the alpha's eyes darken for a split second as if he was in a trance before recovering his senses.

"Come on, bench isn't far." The alpha's voice was rough, breathless.

The man helped Lukas limp to the sidewalk outside the alley, slowly lowered him onto a bench that was haphazardly pushed against the rough brick wall, and stood next to him, arms crossed.

"So what's an omega like you doing walking the streets at night without some form of protection?" the alpha asked, raising his eyebrow.

Lukas once again leaned his head back against the wall, warily side-eyeing the man, before saying, "The dog protected me, didn't it? And I got a good bite on that guy's hand too."

The man looked amused before replying, "Yeah, it would seem you two are cut from the same cloth."

Lukas groaned as he averted his gaze.

The man looked elated. "You must be Lukas. Archer called ahead and told us to expect you."

Lukas looked puzzled before asking, "Us? You and those other people?"

The man shook his head, "I work for Mr. Yorke. Got hired a couple weeks ago. Archer called not long ago and said to keep an eye out for, in his words, 'an angry little omega with a fighter's spirit.' Those other people were just patrons of the bar who heard the commotion."

The man bent next to Lukas and leaned close to his ear, a low voice slipping from his lips. "He also said you might get in trouble on the way. I didn't really understand what he meant at first, and then that scent of yours caught my attention. Then it all made sense."

The silky voice of the alpha so close to him made Lukas shudder, and he felt his cheeks get hot as a low purr followed the stranger's final word.

Lukas leaned his head back against the wall and

watched through half-lidded eyes as the lips of the alpha curled up in a smile. No telling what this guy was thinking if he had picked up on the same thing Lukas had.

Pulling his hat over his unruly hair, Lukas opted to study the man subtly from under the brim as he rested. The alpha stood in the light of a nearby streetlamp, keeping a sharp lookout around them.

He seemed to be in his mid-to-late twenties and had a fierce look about him, but Lukas felt safe around him. The man had shaggy dark red hair, bright silver-blue eyes, pale skin, and a killer smile. He wore the sleek, vintage, black and white uniform the Shattered Gate Bar was known for. His rolled-up sleeves revealed intricate tattoos and small scars.

Lukas thought back to his dreams. *Great, so I'm a psychic now? Perfect.*

Sirens echoed in the distance, ending Lukas' idle thoughts. After a few seconds, the man turned and offered a hand to Lukas.

"Come on, let's get you into the bar. We need to get you patched up. That is, if you'll let me."

Lukas nodded and took the alpha's hand. The man carefully put Lukas' arm over his shoulders and wrapped his arm around Lukas' waist to support him. He turned his head back to the alley.

"Mimosa, come on, girl!"

The dog ran right up to the man before walking next to Lukas, effectively cutting off any escape if he decided he would rather take his chances on the streets. Oh, this alpha and his dog were quite the team alright.

Not that he would try to walk out on the street by himself again right now. Nah, he was quite content being plastered up against the side of this alpha.

Lukas looked up at the man before asking, "So, who do I have to thank for my heroic rescue?"

The alpha looked surprised before replying, "Oh, uh… Owen. Owen Atkins. Nice to meet you. Though I wish it could have been under better circumstances."

Lukas laughed quietly.

"Agreed, Oh-uh Owen."

Owen gave Lukas a look. "Okay, Meep."

"Meep?"

"Hey, if you're going to call me Oh-uh Owen, I am within my rights to call you Meep since that's the first tangible noise you made after that asshat ran off." Owen grinned.

"Fine. Tonight has been embarrassing enough. Thank you, Owen," Lukas whispered.

Owen looked down and smiled. "No problem, Lukas."

CHAPTER 4

*L*ukas had never been inside a bar this late at night before. Even with the patrons gone, it was still bustling with energy. He noticed Mr. Yorke behind the bar, showing off those amazing bartender skills he had heard about. He groaned when a dull pain shot through his body. Damn, he could really use a drink right now.

He felt Owen tense up at his side. He looked up at the alpha and followed his line of sight. There were two rough-looking alphas in the corner of the bar. They looked like they had been ready to leave until they caught sight of the pair entering.

Mr. Yorke noticed the concern in Owen's eyes and quickly pointed them to the breakroom, staring down the alphas as they sat at their table.

Within moments, Lukas found himself on a surprisingly comfy couch. Owen walked over to a small cabinet near some lockers and grabbed some first aid supplies.

Lukas took a second to study the room. It was much bigger than the breakroom back at the diner, and a lot more posh with its classic furniture, colors, and dimmed lights. Most of the furniture looked to be antique. Many different signs and posters hung on the walls, all relics of a bygone era.

He had to hand it to Mr. Yorke, the man knew how to decorate.

Lukas' eyes trailed back toward the door they had come through. "Should we be worried about those other…?"

"Nah, he may look calm and collected all the time, but Mr. Yorke can be a champion heavyweight when he wants to. Trust me, I've known him for years, and I've seen him throw people twice his size to the ground with ease." Owen laughed, clearly fond of whatever memory he was talking about.

Lukas laughed quietly. "Remind me not to get on his bad side."

"Oh, you should see him when he's really pissed off. I watched him stare an unruly alpha into submission pretty recently." Owen chuckled before placing the supplies on the table in front of the couch. "Now, let's take a look at you."

Lukas motioned to his arms, left leg, and back as he tilted his head up. "I hit the wall pretty hard when I was thrown. Had a bit of trouble focusing my vision for a few minutes."

Owen looked concerned. "You could have a concussion. I have to stop the bleeding before I can check. Just don't fall asleep while I'm patching you up. Do whatever you have to to stay awake. It would be a shame if I had to tell Archer your last words were 'wow this is a nice couch.'"

"Okay, Doctor Atkins. I'll keep talking until the cows come home so I don't die on Mr. Yorke's couch," Lukas replied as he pulled his tattered shirt over his head and tossed it onto the back of the couch.

"The real question is, where have the cows gone?" Owen asked with a grin.

"Damn those pesky cows. They go to more parties than I do," Lukas replied, a small smile tugging at his lips.

Owen chuckled and set to work cleaning Lukas' wounds and stopping the bleeding as Lukas began telling stories about the diner and the fair plans.

"…there's going to be lots of bands playing at the venue. To be honest, I'm really excited! I've never been to an outdoor music event before." Lukas spoke quickly, shuddering as the cold, alcohol-soaked rag burned the cuts on his arms.

"…and there's supposed to be a giant, inflatable water slide and slip-and-slides and all sorts of things to go along with the rides." Lukas grinned.

Owen grunted in acknowledgment as he wrapped the gashes on Lukas' arms and leg. Lukas noticed the man's gaze linger on his arms as he tried to sit still. He might not have looked it, but there was definitely taut muscle hidden beneath that old, ragged clothing he had brought from Bellcrest. *So why the hell couldn't I fight that guy off myself?*

"I'm glad you're so excited about it. I'm sure Archer told you a lot about it, and let me say, it's definitely worth all the hype," Owen said.

"So, you've lived, breathed, and experienced this fair? You a local?" Lukas asked.

Owen nodded. "Yeah, born and raised in Boston, but went out to Vegas for a few years. Practiced my trade there and came back here to work with Sheldon. He's an old family friend who needed some help around here, so I obliged."

Lukas was quiet for a moment, wincing as Owen pressed the rag onto a particularly deep cut on his shoulder. He tried to focus on the dog sleeping near the couch.

"So, Mimosa?" Lukas asked with a slight smile. The dog poked her head up at the mention of her name.

Owen chuckled. "Yeah, I brought her with me from Vegas. Someone had dumped her near the bar I was working at. Mimosas were very popular in that bar, and it just seemed right."

"She's a good dog." Lukas smiled before turning his head to look over his shoulder at Owen, trembling when a dull pain shot up his back and neck.

"Yeah, she's a loyal beastie. The best there ever was. Now, let's get your face patched up, and you'll be good to go," Owen said.

Owen stood and moved around to the other side of Lukas and sat down. Lukas' gaze was focused on his wrapped hands. He flexed his fingers every so often to get used to the stiff movement.

"Alright, let's see," Owen murmured, taking the rag and soaking it before holding it up toward Lukas' face. Lukas tilted his head up so Owen could clean the cuts.

Lukas saw Owen's eyes widen as the alpha's breath hitched. Owen's gaze burned into his skin, almost as if the poor guy had just noticed how he looked. He felt goosebumps prickle across his body. The scent from before drifted around them both, a thick cloud of raw sensuality.

"Is everything okay, Owen? Is it that bad?" Lukas asked, ducking his head slightly and averting his eyes.

"Yeah. I mean, no! Damn, let me start over. No, it's not bad, and yeah, everything's okay. Just ignore me. I mean, you're-" Owen stuttered, his voice trailing off.

Lukas raised his eyes, feeling his heart hammer against his chest as he saw the fire in Owen's eyes. It was an intoxicating gaze, and he felt drawn into it. He had wandered so close to the lion's den without an alpha or even an alpha's mark to protect him, and now here he was. Just him and this fascinating, fiery, maybe even foolhardy, alpha.

Calm down. Calm down.

"Don't worry. Everything looks good so far. This is gonna sting pretty bad." Owen soaked the rag in some more alcohol before carefully curling his fingers under Lukas' chin and tilting his head back up. *Damn this alpha and his magic touch.*

"This one may leave a mark. You don't seem like the type to worry about a few scars, but it's a shame…" Owen murmured. "…if I had just been a bit faster, you wouldn't have had to worry about scarring."

Lukas whimpered and tensed when Owen pressed the rag onto a deep cut on his jawline.

"Listen, I know it hurts, but you have to keep pressure on it while I grab some butterfly bandages. If it starts bleeding again, we might have to get you some professional stitches."

"Can do, Doctor Atkins," Lukas quipped before reaching up to take the rag from Owen. Their hands brushed for a moment, causing Lukas to jerk back.

Owen gave him a look, followed by a smile. "You're breaking my heart. I hope I'm not that repulsive," he joked before covering the smaller cuts on Lukas' face.

"No. No, it's just… I'm not used to– … a lot has happened tonight, and you're–" Lukas trailed off. He felt his face getting warm.

"I know. I'm the big, scary alpha who picked you up off the street while you were vulnerable. Trust me,

I know. You don't have to worry. I know you haven't known me for long, but I'm not like that one on the street, I promise you," Owen whispered, raising his eyes to look into Lukas'.

Lukas felt goosebumps rising on his skin as he locked eyes with Owen. Shivers ran across his body as every part of him hummed with energy. Owen's fingers lightly touching his face left behind a searing heat as he got lost in those steely eyes. *Uh-oh.*

The tension was broken when an impossibly loud knock came on the door of the bar. Lukas realized he had leaned a bit closer to Owen and quickly shrunk back into the couch, averting his eyes.

"Is everything all right in there, Owen? Is your friend okay? May I come in?" came a voice from outside.

Lukas looked down at the couch before closing his eyes and shivering.

Owen looked disappointed for a split second and then relieved. "Is it all right if he comes in?"

Lukas nodded before Owen replied, "Yes, sir. Everything is alright now. Please, come in."

The door opened with a creak as Mr. Yorke stepped in, closing it behind him.

"I went ahead and closed the bar a bit early, so you can stay back here as long as you need to, boys," Mr. Yorke said. He walked over and put his hands on the back of the couch, balancing his weight on it.

Lukas looked concerned. "You'll lose out on a lot of money doing that, Mr. Yorke. Are you sure?"

"Bah, there are a hundred other places where they can go get drunk for a night. Frankly, I'm more concerned about people like you that need help," Mr. Yorke replied.

"I really appreciate it, sir." Lukas' voice was low and humble.

"So what happened out there? I saw numerous people run out and then you came waltzing in with poor Lukas slung across your shoulder!" Mr. Yorke exclaimed, glancing at Owen before pausing on Lukas.

"Surely you noticed that almost every person who ran out was an alpha?" Owen asked in a quiet tone.

Mr. Yorke sat down at his nearby desk. "Ah, yes, that makes sense. In most cases, I would supply some scent blocker. However, at the speed those alphas ran out of here, I'd say that…"

Owen nodded. "Yeah. Won't do much good now."

Lukas looked weary before removing the rag from his jaw and letting Owen plaster some butterfly bandages over the wound.

"Archer was telling me the same thing before I left, saying that… well, that this one is different. Also said I should stay home when it finally hits. I've been here for five years, and he's never said anything about my scent until tonight. I wonder what changed?"

Lukas saw Owen tense as he heard those words.

Mr. Yorke took a breath before saying, "Lad, that means your scent is just becoming stronger than whatever is in those blockers. As Archer already said, it will be very dangerous for you to go out when your next heat hits."

"But what's so dangerous about this heat?" Lukas asked.

"In short, you're experiencing something rare. Means you caught a special scent of something or someone, and your body is responding in kind. In a city this large, it's always hard to determine where you came into contact with that scent," Mr. Yorke continued. "But when your next heat does hit, if an alpha catches scent of you, and they aren't strong enough to control themselves, they'd enter into a frenzy, and you wouldn't be able to stop them. Rather, your own body wouldn't let you."

Lukas heard Owen make a noise at the back of his throat quietly before he turned his attention back to Lukas' wrist.

It made sense now. Lukas didn't have to guess what had triggered this reaction in his body. His mind was racing as he leaned sideways against the back of the couch. Earlier, he had thought he didn't need to be rescued, that he could take care of himself. Proven wrong, he wavered.

Give in. Be a good little omega. A strong alpha is so close. He'll take care of you. Lose yourself in his scent, his embrace. Take it all in.

No. He wasn't going to give in. He could handle this himself. So it would be a bit rougher than his last heats, no biggie. He just needed more supplies since he would be home the entire time.

After a moment, Mr. Yorke sighed and stood.

"Just be careful, lad. Now, I'll let Owen finish patching you up. You look like you're about to pass out on that couch. I'll get you two something to eat." Mr. Yorke headed back to the now empty bar.

Owen carefully re-wrapped a spot on Lukas' wrist. "You good?"

"Yeah, thank you," Lukas replied with a yawn.

Owen looked worried before whispering, "Don't you dare fall asleep. I still have to make sure you don't have a concussion."

"Might have to slap me around a little bit, Doctor Atkins. This couch is mighty comfortable," Lukas said quietly with a sleepy smile. "Just know, I might fight back."

Owen chuckled, nodding before saying, "Oh, trust me, I saw *first-hand* the kind of damage you can do."

A slow smile tugged at Owen's lips. "Get it?"

Lukas thought back to what Owen said before sighing and dipping his head down. His hand slowly covered his face before moving down to his mouth.

"Noooo, you did not just–" A quiet snicker escaped from behind Lukas' hand.

Owen threw his arm over the back of the couch, smiling.

They heard the door open once again, and Mr. Yorke said, "I'll be cleaning up out here until you two are ready to go. Just shut off the lights as you come out, Owen."

"Alright, Boss," Owen replied before looking back at Lukas. "Right. Let's get you finished up. Stay seated here and follow the light with your eyes, okay?"

Owen took out a small flashlight from the first aid kit and crouched in front of Lukas. He concentrated carefully while he shined it into Lukas' eyes before putting it away and slowly moving his finger across Lukas' field of vision. Lukas forced himself to focus on the finger instead of the man behind it.

"Okay, looking good. Now go ahead and try to stand up. Use me for support if you need to," Owen stood up and offered an arm to Lukas.

Lukas stood, legs shaking a bit from sitting on them, and promptly grabbed Owen's shoulder to steady himself. He felt an arm reach around to support his waist.

"Damn it," Lukas whispered, voice laced with pain.

Owen held Lukas. "I'll let Mr. Yorke know to call Archer and tell him you won't be in tomorrow."

"No need. We already agreed we're all taking a day off tomorrow. I just need to get home and rest," Lukas replied, eyes half-lidded.

"Then I'm taking you home. No way I'm going to let you ride a cramped bus in your condition," Owen replied before helping Lukas sit on the couch again.

"I'll let Mr. Yorke know we're ready to go. If you give me the outline and supply list, I'll put them on his desk, and we can head out."

Lukas felt a cold chill all over his body.

"I was holding them when I was... ah shit..." Lukas' voice trailed off.

"Probably long gone by now." Owen sat next to Lukas. "It's nothing. We can get Archer to print out another copy later."

"Yeah, that should be fine," Lukas replied with relief in his voice.

Owen leaned his head against the back of the couch, taking in a deep breath and staring at the ceiling for a few seconds before standing.

"Let's get you home. It's already past one. Come on."

Lukas stood, supported once more by Owen, and they walked out to the bar where Mr. Yorke was waiting. After telling the man about the outline and supply list, they left the bar and walked to Owen's car.

Within a few minutes, they were on the street, Lukas in the front seat, and Mimosa in the back. Owen noticed that Lukas was still fighting sleep.

"You can sleep now if you need to. You've checked out of the Shattered Gate Hospital with a clean bill of health."

Lukas yawned. "You've already done a lot for me tonight. If I fall asleep in this car, I won't wake up for a good ten hours, probably more. You'll have to carry me up the stairs to my room once we get to my place."

Owen chuckled before going silent. A stoplight

changed to red, and he pulled to a stop. The chatter of the people in the crosswalk ahead of them filled the silence. Nearby, another driver revved their engine, waiting for the moment the light turned green.

Owen rolled up the windows, blocking out the noises of the city. "I hope I didn't scare you too much in that alley."

Lukas was shocked. Usually, alphas didn't care much about the effect their presence had on others. They were large and in charge and wanted everyone to know that.

"Honestly, I was terrified at first, but I think your scent really helped. Once I calmed down, I realized something. It was familiar, you see," Lukas replied, thankful the darkness of the car hid his flushed face.

Owen sighed. "I think a few alphas in this town have really made a bad name for all of us."

The rest of the ride was silent. It wasn't long before they pulled up in front of Lukas' home.

Owen came around and opened the door for Lukas, offering his hand.

Making their way to the steps, Lukas suddenly spoke up. "Hey, hang on, I need to say a few things before you go."

They sat down on the front steps, looking out at the buildings and cars in silence, while Lukas gathered his thoughts.

"Words can't express how thankful I am to you, Owen. From the day I moved here, I was so worried that everybody would be lookin' out for number one. I never thought I'd find such kindness here. Thank you for provin' me wrong." Lukas' Southern drawl was apparent, each word dripping with sincerity.

"You're welcome. I just wish we could have met in

a situation that didn't involve you getting hurt like that," Owen replied quietly.

Owen seemed nervous, unsure of what to say. A moment of silence passed.

"Can we trade numbers? I need to be able to contact you about the fair," Owen said. "…but I wouldn't mind having your number so I can talk with you outside of fair planning." Owen smiled softly.

Lukas tensed before his body heated up. He scooted closer and leaned into Owen's side.

Numbers traded, Owen stood up, bringing Lukas up with him.

"Thank you again, Owen. I'll be in touch." Lukas shakily stood. "I'll get that copy of the plans to you and Mr. Yorke as soon as possible," he said, hand on the doorknob.

Owen smiled before replying, "I better not see you out and about tomorrow. You need to rest, first and foremost. If you need anything, please call me. In fact, call me for any reason."

"At ease, Doctor Atkins. I feel like I could sleep for days right now." Lukas laughed.

"Is it all right if I swing by tomorrow before work to check on you?" Owen asked.

Lukas looked surprised and then smiled. "I would like that very much."

"Good. I'll be by around six tomorrow evening. Sleep well, Lukas," Owen replied in a soft tone.

"Goodnight, Owen. Be safe heading home," Lukas whispered. He watched Owen walk back to his car and drive off before stepping inside and closing the door behind him.

Lukas sank to the floor once the door was closed. He heard Miss Mulberry plodding down the stairs, meowing, before climbing into his lap.

He idly stroked his fingers through the cat's long fur, thinking about the events of the day. So much had happened in such a short amount of time, and at the center of it all was this handsome, caring, kind alpha.

Lukas let out a small sigh. "Yep. I'm doomed."

arm sunlight streamed through the windows as Lukas looked at the clock.

"Already past noon, huh? Guess I was out really late last night." Lukas yawned and sat up in his bed. Miss Mulberry stretched at his feet.

His body felt hotter and tenser than it usually did in the week leading up to his heat. A dull pain pulsed through his body, affecting every last bit of him.

"Guess it's true, huh? Can't wait for this to hit," he whispered sarcastically. "Damn, all this because of his scent?"

His thoughts wandered back to Owen. He might have looked mean and rough, but he really was an upstanding guy.

He could really pull off that bar outfit too. It was his style. That, and it hugged him in *just* the right places.

Miss Mulberry meowed from the doorway of the bedroom.

Lukas looked at her from the bed as a dreadful thought crossed his mind.

"Poor thing, you're probably starving. Did I even feed you last night?

He got up out of bed as quickly as his battered body would allow him to and slowly hobbled to the doorway.

"I must have. Otherwise, you would have been walking on me all night. I swear you're tenderizing me for a later date." Lukas chuckled.

After filling her food dish, he sat at the kitchen table and looked at his phone.

"Two missed calls from Archer and four unread messages. Let's see."

Checking the messages first, he saw one message from Archer, one from Sienna, one from Sawyer, and the last one…

"From Owen?"

Wakey wakey. I hope you're able to move without much pain this morning. Hopefully, I was gentle enough with you. You should call Archer and let him know how you're doing. He's really worried about you.

Lukas read the message unhurriedly. He felt his cheeks warm up as he reread the text. What the hell was up with that wording?

"He did that on purpose," Lukas whispered to himself. That damn alpha. He felt heat on his face for a brief second before his gaze softened. No matter what he was thinking, or how he rebelled against his own body, he was thankful for that damn alpha.

He looked for Archer's name in his contacts and dialed the number.

The phone rang precisely half a ring before Archer picked up. Lukas didn't have time to say anything before Archer started freaking out.

"Lukas, are you okay? How are you feeling? I was so worried after you left the diner and then I got that call from Mr. Yorke! Shit, what were you thinking? If Owen had been a minute later–" Lukas had to hold the phone away from his ear.

After a moment of silence, Lukas tentatively held the phone back to his ear.

"I'm hurting, but I've been well taken care of thanks to Owen. He'll be stopping by later tonight to check on me."

Archer sighed, "I still can't believe you. I told you it was dangerous, and what did you do? You decided to flounce on outside without a care in the world."

"Really, Boss, it's okay now. Lesson learned. I'm sorry I worried you. I'm glad you called ahead to the bar, though," Lukas said.

"I'll have to send a thank you to Mr. Yorke and tell him to give that man a raise. I don't care if he just started, that man deserves a bigger paycheck, a brand-new car, or something," Archer replied with a stressed sigh.

The two men talked for a while longer before Lukas suddenly remembered something.

"Hey, last night when I was... I was reading the plans for the fair, and they kind of..." his voice trailed off, remembering the events of last night.

"Oh, don't worry about that, Owen let me know what happened. I already sent Sienna over to drop off another copy with Mr. Yorke since she was already in the area," Archer said.

Lukas heaved a sigh of relief. "Alright. And I'll work on the pies and cakes as soon as I can."

"I'll get you Mr. Yorke's number in case you need to get a hold of him. I can't wait to try all those tasty treats," Archer said dreamily.

"On a side note, could you ask Mr. Yorke what sort of sweets Owen likes? I want to bake him something. And Mr. Yorke too. They deserve good homemade treats..." Lukas' voice trailed off as he thought about Owen enjoying some treats he put his heart into.

"Well, I know for a fact Mr. Yorke loves anything with pecans in it, but I'll get back to you on what Owen likes. For now, you should rest. I'll sic Sienna on you if you don't," Archer said forcefully.

Lukas laughed. "You're no Doctor Atkins, but I'll take your advice. Is the diner going to be open tomorrow?"

"Yeah, it'll be open. If you need more days off, just let me know. We need you in tip-top shape for the Heated Hullabaloo," Archer replied.

"Okay, Boss. I'll let you know. Talk to you later." Lukas' gaze drifted to the clock hanging above the kitchen table.

"See you soon, Lukas," Archer ended the call with a cheerful tone.

THE HOURS FLEW BY. LUKAS FOCUSED ON CLEANING UP his home before Owen came over. Miss Mulberry sat in the window in the bedroom, looking outside.

While folding some laundry on the bed, Lukas heard Miss Mulberry meow. She was carefully watching a bug in the plants in the window boxes, waiting to strike.

"I never got the chance to water yesterday," Lukas murmured under his breath.

Walking over to his dresser, he quickly took out some worn jeans and an old, light green plaid shirt. He changed into the tattered clothing and went into the kitchen and grabbed his small watering can. Opening the window, he looked over the small plants.

"Ah, you bloomed quite a bit," Lukas whispered, fingers running over the petals of a purple petunia. "About time."

He let the water sprinkle over the plants, leaving translucent specks that caught the light of the sun.

He admired the flowers for a moment before closing the window. He put away his small watering can under the sink. He was about to walk up the stairs to his roof when the doorbell rang.

"Six already?" Lukas gasped, looking at the clock.

He walked to the entryway, straightening the collar on his shirt and running his hand through his hair. He quickly replaced his hat before opening the door.

As expected, there stood Owen. The man was in casual clothes instead of the dapper duds he'd worn yesterday at the bar.

He noticed the look of confusion on Lukas' face and explained, "Mr. Yorke let me have the night off. I brought Mexican food if you're hungry."

Owen held up two bags of steaming hot food.

Lukas' mouth watered.

"Archer told you this was my favorite, didn't he? Wow."

Owen laughed. "Yeah, he said you have a huge appreciation for Mexican food, and there's this amazing joint near my apartment. I figured I'd pick some up for us."

"Please, come on in. It's a bit of a mess, but I hope it's okay." Lukas stepped back so Owen could enter.

Lukas heard the man's breath hitch as he walked into the entryway.

"What's wrong? I didn't think my house was that dirty," Lukas joked, quietly closing the door behind them.

"Yeah, yeah, I'm good. Just… you have a gorgeous home, Lukas." Owen looked around in amazement. A meow came from upstairs, and Owen froze.

At that moment, Miss Mulberry came plodding

down the stairs, drawn by the new voice. Owen's mouth dropped a bit.

"And that is the cutest cat I have ever seen," Owen whispered, starstruck.

Lukas laughed before taking a few steps, scooping the little bundle of fluff into his arms, and walking back to Owen.

"Come on, let's put the food down in the kitchen. I'll grab us a couple of drinks and then you can hold her if you want."

"Nothing like good food, the good company of friends… and Jack Daniels." Owen sighed, taking a quick drink. "You know, we'll have to drop by the bar at some point, and I can make you some drinks that will really blow your mind."

The time passed quickly, each man lost in the company of the other. It was about seven-thirty when Lukas remembered something.

"Damn, it's this late, and I still haven't watered my garden." He stood up, gathering the tin trays from their meal. He quickly washed and dried them, then tucked them under his arm.

"Need some help?" Owen asked.

"Sure. Follow me, squire." Lukas motioned with his free hand.

Lukas felt Owen follow him closely around the corner to the front entrance. As he headed up the first steps, a shine on the wall caught his eye. Sunlight was streaming in through the glass of the front door and reflecting off a few framed pictures hanging on the wall.

He turned when he didn't hear the alpha's heavy steps behind him and caught a glimpse of Owen staring at an old family photo. He waited nearby, watching as Owen's gaze trailed to the scattered pictures of farm animals, his old family farmhouse, and Miss Mulberry in her early years.

"It's a wall full of memories. I can tell you all about them later, if you'd like." Lukas chuckled from his spot on the stairway, smiling as he looked at the frames. "But first, the garden."

A faint smile appeared on Owen's face as he looked up at Lukas, as if he finally realized they were heading upstairs.

"And here I was heading toward the front door. Whatever was I thinking?" he asked, raising his eyebrow.

Lukas' lips turned up in a smile before he walked up one last dark flight of stairs that led to the roof. He opened the door, and the light of the sunset filled the dim stairwell.

Lukas stepped back as he watched Owen step into the center of the garden. The man looked like he was in a trance, suddenly surrounded by a whole new world. Lukas turned and saw the Charles River sparkling in the last bit of sunlight. The pleasant scent of flowers hit him, blocking out the smoke of the city. Standing among it all was this handsome alpha. It was like something out of a fairy tale.

"Lukas, this is amazing." Owen stood in awe, looking at the splashes of color painted across the patio.

"My home away from home," Lukas whispered, leading Owen under the arch he had built. It was covered in flowering vines that added a bit of shade to the area. Nearby, a wooden wind chime caught the breeze, helping to block out the hubbub of the city. There were berry bushes planted in raised beds near the edge of the building with trellis walls supporting them.

"So, what all do you have up here?" Owen questioned, looking around in astonishment.

"Mostly vegetables. They're still growing, but I have tomatoes, squash, zucchini, and peppers in this bed. In this one, kale and snow peas," Lukas replied, pointing out each plant type.

"You saw all the berries on the trellis walls. I have blueberries, blackberries, and strawberries," Lukas added.

"What about that bed?" Owen asked, looking back toward the door they had come through. There was a small bed in the area to the right of the doorway.

"Mostly flowers. My friend Sawyer is a florist, so he sometimes plants different kinds here. I think there are snapdragons, petunias, and columbine right now." Lukas led Owen over to the small flowerbed.

He thought for a moment before whispering, "We also planted catnip in there. Use that info as you will."

Owen's eyes lit up as Lukas walked over to the raised beds.

"I just need to check on everything before it gets dark. There's a bench by the berry bushes if you want to sit for a while. You know, enjoy the nice view up here," Lukas walked to each of the beds, feeling the soil.

Thankfully, it must have rained last night sometime after he got home. The soil was still damp enough that he didn't have to worry about watering any of the plants.

Grabbing a small pruner off a table near the doorway, he set to work clipping off dead branches and cleaning up the plants.

Owen walked around, admiring the hard work that had been put into the garden space.

Lukas cut small holes in the tins he'd brought up and threaded twine through them. He carefully hung them near his raised beds, biting his lip in concentration as he made sure they would stay in place.

"What are those for?" Owen asked.

Lukas grinned before saying, "This is my patented hillbilly pest control system."

"Damn. So, you eat the Mexican food, the Mexican food stops birds from eating your crops, the crops get made into more delicious food for everyone, and then you get enough money to buy more Mexican food. Ah, the circle of life," Owen quipped.

Lukas laughed, grabbing a small basket from the table, a small smile crossing his face as he carefully examined berries before plucking them and putting them in the basket.

"So, I heard you're going to be doing a lot of baking for the Hullabaloo. Does that mean this garden is going to supply most of the treats?" Owen asked.

"Yeah, most of these berries will be made into pies, tarts, dumplings, and cakes. I'm just happy this garden is doing so well. I was worried I might have lost my green thumb."

Owen looked at Lukas.

"What do you mean?"

A sad smile crossed Lukas' face. "Well, it's been a long time since I left North Carolina, and this is the first garden I've done on my own, even before moving here. My parents owned a farm, you see, and we always had a thriving garden, but…"

He saw Owen stop in his tracks.

"…they died in a car accident when I was thirteen. My older brother, Colton, was seventeen," Lukas continued. "Damn, it's been ten years already."

He saw Owen carefully, almost cautiously, step

forward before asking, "So what happened to you and your brother?"

"Colton and I bounced around from foster home to foster home until he turned eighteen. At that point, he was able to access the money our parents left for us. I stayed with him in a small apartment until I turned eighteen, then I left with my share. I couldn't be a burden on him any longer than I already had been." Lukas averted his gaze.

"How did you end up here? You're a long way from home. Do you have any family here?"

"Nah, just me. Last time I talked to him, my brother was living in Atlanta. Well, not Atlanta, but a small community on the outskirts. My Ma actually lived here, in Boston, before she met Pa. This was her old place. She sold it to a family friend when she moved down to be with Pa," Lukas said. "I got lucky, though. Her friend found out I was looking for a place to stay, and she's letting me stay here for a fair price."

He felt Owen's gaze on him. Alarm bells went off in his head. *Too much, too smoldering, too exposed.* Lukas trailed his fingers across the brim of his old, faded tan, ball cap before pulling it down to hide his face from the alpha.

"And what about this cap? I haven't seen you go anywhere without it."

"It was my Pa's. Wore it every day when he went out to work on the farm."

A pitiful, shuddering sigh escaped Lukas' lips as he felt Owen's fingers tentatively touch his free hand, slowly intertwining their fingers together.

"You know, Ma loved it up here just as much as she did back home. Every year, she talked about bringing us all up here for a vacation. She wanted to show us the world she knew before she settled down with Pa, but every year it was always pushed off. There was always something to do on the farm, something with school, always something. And now–"

Lukas' voice wavered as he spoke up. "I'm sorry. I'm making a fool of myself. I just tried for so long to keep it to myself and now…"

Lukas suddenly felt himself pulled into a tight hug. He tensed against Owen before a choked noise escaped his lips. He let his arms encircle the alpha and curled his fingers into the rough fabric of the man's shirt.

Ah, shit. Yep, I'm done for.

"You're no fool, Lukas. You have beaten the odds. You're living your own life despite what you've been through. You have good memories of your family, and you're making new memories here. This garden, this piece of art right here? It connects you to the past and the future, and the future is looking quite bright from where I'm standing."

Lukas was quiet for a time, leaning into the warmth of the alpha before whispering, "You're right. I like that. A connection to the past and the future."

Warmth. Strength. Submit to him. His omega voice buzzed in his head, sending waves of warmth down his spine. Lukas took a deep breath, feeling Owen shift next to him.

It had gotten late, and the roof was only lit by the remnants of the sunset. Lukas felt Owen's arm resting on the back of the bench, his fingers ever-so-slightly brushing against the omega's shoulder. Looking up at the alpha, Lukas felt his breath hitch. Owen's eyes were really bright now, almost silver. But no matter how tough and cold those eyes seemed, Lukas felt heat well up inside him every time he found them focused on him.

Damn it. I want to– ...but it's too soon, isn't it?

Lukas' thoughts were interrupted by a muffled meow at the door.

"Oh no, we've been caught." Owen sighed before smiling.

"I guess we have been out here for a while," Lukas replied with a laugh. "Come on, she may just die without attention."

"We can't let anything happen to that innocent creature! Come, we will cuddle her." Owen took Lukas' hand in his and walked back to the door.

Lukas let himself be hauled back downstairs, Miss Mulberry following.

"So, uh, how would you feel about staying a bit longer for dessert? I can bake something fresh," Lukas said. "I mean, if you have to go, it's–

"I would love to. Stay, that is. Dessert sounds great right now."

A smile appeared on Lukas' flushed face. "So, what's your favorite treat?"

Owen instantly stated, "I would swim across the Charles River in the dead of winter for a fresh apple dumpling with a ton of cinnamon."

"Well, come on, partner. We have a lot of work to do." Lukas laughed before motioning for Owen to follow him into the kitchen.

CHAPTER 6

"Don't you throw that banana. Don't you do it," a gruff voice growled.

"You just watch me," came a low, challenging voice.

"No, I'm right behind you! You'll kill me, and then the evil ones will win," the first voice pleaded.

"Sayonara, partner," the second voice cackled.

The world seemed to go in slow motion as the banana was dropped onto the road. A pair of drivers on one side of the split-screen hit the peel and spun out of control into a river. Many other pairs sped past to the finish line. Owen looked absolutely devastated as he watched the results play out on the screen.

Lukas doubled over on the couch, laughing.

"You came in second; you're okay," he said through giggles.

Owen turned and looked at Lukas in despair. "No, Lukas, I don't think you understand the gravity of this situation. Look at the smug look on that turtle's face. Evil has prevailed!"

"Well, you better stock the bunker, city-slicker." Lukas tried to catch his breath.

"I will not hunker down. I will fight!" Owen declared. "Lukas, we'll fight for the fate of the world. Get your weed killer because you're going after the weird plant thing while I get the angry turtle. We got this."

Owen threw his arm over the back of the couch and looked at the clock on the wall. "It's a little past two. Do you want to go out for lunch? My treat."

It had been four days since Lukas was attacked. He was still sore, and he had eventually had to go get stitches after a wound on his arm opened back up, but he knew he had to get out of the house soon.

Lukas thought for a moment and nodded. "Hell yeah, where to?"

Owen smiled and stood, pulling Lukas up with him and grabbing his wallet and keys off the table.

"You'll see. I have a suspicious feeling you'll love it."

THE DINER SEEMED NO WORSE FOR WEAR. AS OWEN helped him out of the car, he saw Archer's truck and Sienna's van parked in the employee section. He wondered if they knew he was coming.

He got his answer when he was immediately spotted by a surprised Archer. Nearby, Sienna and someone he had never seen before were rushing to and fro delivering orders.

"There he is, the star of the show!" Archer yelled across the diner, causing the customers to smile and look toward the door.

Lukas cringed a bit before waving at Archer. His head still hurt, and he wasn't fond of the stares from the customers.

"Hey, Boss. Glad to be here." Lukas smiled,

gingerly walking behind the counter and clapping Archer on the shoulder.

"Glad you're feeling a bit better, Lukas," came a cheery voice from behind him.

An older female omega stood there, balancing a tray on one hand and smiling at Lukas. She sported a refined retro uniform that made her blend in with the old-fashioned diner, big hair and all. Her dark skin practically glowed with positive energy, and her smile lit up the room. She stepped forward, giving him a quick hug before looking him up and down, eyeing the stitches in his arm.

The beautiful woman standing before him was a huge blessing. They had been friends for years before she moved to Boston to be near her parents, and they regularly kept in touch online. She was an angel in disguise, this much he knew, because when he suddenly moved up to Boston with no plan what-so-ever, she helped him out, no questions asked.

"Hey, Sienna. It's good to be back. How's Hazel feeling?" Lukas questioned.

Sienna looked relieved. "I got her to the doctor and got some medicine in her, so she was finally able to get some sleep. Doctor said it was one of the worst bouts of strep she'd ever seen. How about you? Are you sure you're feeling good enough to be here?"

"I'm still sore and bruised, but I'll go insane if I'm stuck in the house for much longer," Lukas replied.

Archer called out to the new guy, motioning him toward a tray full of food that was ready to go out before darting over to the oven to pull out another dish.

Sienna looked toward Owen. "And who is this? Is this the guy who…?"

Lukas smiled, looking toward Owen, "Yeah, this is

Owen. He's the one who saved my ass and patched me up."

"And thus, his ass was saved. No harm came to it." Owen grinned.

Lukas felt his face get hot as Archer laughed and turned to Owen.

"I have to thank you for getting our favorite little troublemaker out of trouble," Archer said, shaking Owen's hand.

Owen nodded before saying, "He's definitely a fighter, like you said. He managed to hold off that guy until I got there."

He turned to Sienna, bowing. "You have trained him well."

Sienna smiled at Owen, giving him a nod before picking up her tray and menus.

"Damn right, I did. Follow me right this way, boys. We'll get you the best seat in the house."

Owen stretched, exhaling a deep breath as he relaxed. He leaned down to whisper to Lukas, "I'm gonna hit the restroom. I'll be back in a few."

Nodding, Lukas replied, "Don't take too long. I'll order for both of us and finish both meals, I promise you."

A look of shock crossed Owen's features before he held a hand to his chest.

"A man after my own heart. I trust you'll order only the best." He winked before walking off in the direction of the restrooms.

The moment Owen left, the new guy came up to the front of the diner, his gaze flitting between Lukas and the floor. Lukas paused, feeling his nose twitch as he tried to figure out what was wrong with the other man. The man swallowed hard, licking his lips before trying to speak. *Poor guy is so nervous. Time to lay on the Southern charm.*

Lukas turned and smiled, holding out his hand. "Hey, don't believe we've met. You a new hire?"

The stranger seemed shocked at the sudden introduction, but took Lukas' hand and shook it, his eyes now completely focused on the floor.

"Y-yes, sir. I'm Aaron Hudson. Started on just a couple days ago. Nice to meet you."

"Thought we could use some more help with the fair getting closer. All the colleges have let out for the summer, and he was looking for something part-time whenever school starts back up. This is his first serving job, but he's a fast learner." Archer quickly threw together a sandwich for an order.

"Thank you, sir," Aaron replied. "I'm still a little nervous, but everyone has been very cordial with me so far."

Archer smiled. "So, Aaron, Lukas will only be doing half days for a while once he gets back, but he can show you some tips and tricks while he's here. After he's feeling better, he's going to be making a lot of treats for the Heated Hullabaloo."

Sienna chimed in, "Yeah, he's one of the best cooks I know. The fair will have some pretty amazing food between him, Archer, and Mr. Yorke."

Aaron looked up at Lukas, and a small smile formed on his lips. "I'm looking forward to it, sir."

Lukas snickered, "You don't have to call me 'sir.' We're around the same age, I'm sure."

A look of shock crossed Aaron's face. "Sorry, sometimes it just slips out. My mee-maw was strict on manners like that."

"Hey, Aaron, got another order for you, let's hop to it!" Archer called from behind the counter.

Aaron rushed over, waving to Lukas and Sienna as they walked to the booths at the back of the diner.

"He seems like a good kid. Hard worker, at the

very least, and he seemed very happy to meet you, too. Toughest thing has been making sure he takes his eyes off the ground every now and then," Sienna giggled.

"Here's hoping he works out well for the diner. It's been getting a bit too crazy around here for my liking." Lukas gazed back at the counter, catching the eyes of Aaron, who waved to the pair with a smile.

"...AND IF YOU WANT TO BE A SUPER SERVER, YOU MAKE friends with your regulars. Archer comes up with all sorts of new dishes, so learn what they like and make recommendations for the new selections based on that info. Trust me." Lukas took a bite of his sandwich as Aaron laid out menus on a nearby table.

"You seem close with a lot of the people here," Aaron replied.

Lukas paused, raising an eyebrow. *What's with that face? He looks... sad? Irritated, maybe?*

"Yeah, a lot of good people frequent this place, and it's always fun when Mrs. Xian brings her three kiddos in." Lukas laughed to himself as he remembered Mei and Jin tackling him to the floor.

Lukas thought for a moment before saying in a sinister voice, "There is one lady you have to watch out for though."

Owen's gaze shot across the table to Lukas as Aaron took a step back. It was as if they felt the very air around Lukas change.

"W-who would that be?" Aaron stuttered.

Lukas faked a shudder and looked Aaron in the eyes. At that moment, as if planned, the door to the diner opened, and a sing-song voice pierced the air.

"Lukas!"

Aaron saw Lukas cringe and turn around in his

seat. Within a moment, Lukas was wrapped in a hug by a deceptively firm grip.

A woman's voice rang out, "Lukas, I'm so glad you're back! Are you okay, sweetie? I was so worried about you. We all were."

A muffled groan came from Lukas. "I'm fine, Ms. Newman. It's good to see you too."

Archer watched with amusement from the counter.

Lukas thought for a moment. "Wait. We?"

As the minutes passed, more customers came trickling into the diner and came over to talk to Lukas, checking up on him since he hadn't been at the diner for a few days.

Owen smiled, watching the number of people around their booth grow, "Well, I'll be damned. You have your own fan club, Lukas. Means there's more competition now." He smiled gently, taking a long sip of his soda.

A few giggles came from the crowd. Owen looked toward Ms. Newman and was shocked by her expression.

"Lukas, you found someone you like?" Ms. Newman shifted her gaze back toward Lukas.

A pleasant pink hue covered Lukas' cheeks as he looked across the table toward Owen, "I'm sure you heard what happened from Archer. This is Owen. He's the one who saved me and fixed me up."

Ms. Newman looked positively pleased with the situation, clapping her hands together and smiling. "You done good, Owen. This diner just isn't the same without our little Lukas."

Murmurs of agreement came from the other customers crowding the area around the booth. Owen looked a bit sheepish as he scratched the back of his head and smiled.

Suddenly, there was a clatter across the diner. Gazes flitted to the front, where Aaron had suddenly dropped a tray of glasses on the counter, causing a number to tip and fall to the floor.

Lukas yelled out, "Don't try to–!"

His warning came too late. Aaron dove to catch a few of the stray glasses before they shattered. A yelp came from the crouched figure.

Lukas jumped up from the booth and rushed over to help as Archer's voice echoed across the diner, "What happened? Everyone okay?"

Aaron looked positively mortified. Lukas squatted next to him, catching the sharp metallic scent of blood. Lukas looked down and saw a gash across Aaron's palm and fingers.

"Hey, don't worry about it, Aaron. I can patch this up easy," Lukas whispered to the newbie.

Lukas carefully took Aaron's hand, holding it flat to survey the damage. He leaned closer to his injured co-worker, and saw the man tense up. Shocks ran through his body as he felt Aaron's rough hand grasp his wrist.

"I appreciate it, but you don't have to worry about me. I've dealt with bad cuts like this before." Aaron furrowed his brow.

"Hush. I'm not about to let you bleed out on the floor," Lukas said forcefully.

Lukas looked up, feeling Aaron's eyes burning into him. They were a startling amber color, warm and inviting to most, but something in them made Lukas' gut twist.

Danger. Wait, danger? Why is he–?

Aaron was quiet for a moment before a light flush flashed across his face. He tilted his lips up in a soft smile, taking in a deep breath.

"You're too kind for your own good," Aaron spoke quietly, almost as if he were talking to himself.

Lukas helped Aaron to his feet, lightly patting the taller man's back. *I'm freaking out over nothing.*

EVENTUALLY, THE LUNCH CROWD THINNED, AND Sienna and Aaron got to slow down a bit. Archer decided to go ahead and send Aaron home for the day, closing the back door behind him as he walked out into the parking lot.

Owen leaned closer to Lukas, showing him something on his phone before raising his head to yell to Sienna. The two had really become fast friends within the past hour. The waitress was taking it upon herself to torment Owen every now and then from the other side of the diner.

Lukas idly glanced out the window for a moment and saw Aaron freeze mid-step, staring back at the pair. His face was sad, almost. The other man tensed for a moment before turning and powerwalking out of sight.

Lukas tilted his head. *What was that all about?* He was startled as Sienna came over to sit on the opposite side of their booth.

Sienna studied the couple for a moment before saying, "We've really missed you here, Lukas. I know it's crazy with the fair and all, but you should stay home if you're still hurting."

Lukas chuckled, "Don't worry about me, Sienna. You've got enough to worry about with Hazel, you don't have to add me to the list. Besides, I have Doctor Atkins here."

Owen, who was sipping his soda, nodded and tried to smile without spilling his drink.

Nodding, Sienna seemed a bit lost in thought.

"Lukas, you should go check in with Archer. He's been wanting to talk over some fair things with you."

"Will do. I'll be right back," Lukas replied, wiggling out of the booth. He knew what was coming. Sienna did with every alpha that was around him for long periods of time, a bit of a scare-tactic that she used to filter out the bad apples.

Left alone with Sienna, he heard Owen begin to speak, "So, how long have you been workin–"

He was cut off mid-sentence by Sienna, who motioned for him to be quiet for a moment.

"Listen, you seem like a really nice guy. I can tell Lukas adores you. But you should know he's been through a lot of shit, so I'm only going to say this once."

Sienna leaned closer and lowered her voice.

"I'm a woman who's normally made of sunshine and rainbows, but if you hurt him... well, did you know it only takes a few bags of lime?"

Owen gulped before asking, "For what?"

Sienna put her elbows on the table, leaning onto them while threading her fingers together under her chin before whispering, "To dispose of common filth, of course."

With this, her eyes shot up to make contact with Owen's.

A cold ball of dread settled in Owen's stomach before he nodded.

"I understand."

Sienna beamed, once again returning to her caring mom attitude.

"Good. You take good care of our boy, okay? He's a breath of fresh air in this city, and he needs someone to protect and cherish him."

Looking delighted, Owen agreed, "I will guard him against all harm. I promise."

Lukas felt his cheeks warm up as a stupid smile flashed across his face.

As more customers trickled in, Sienna stood, "I'm holding you to that promise. It was nice meeting you, Owen. Take care and make sure Lukas rests properly. Bruised just isn't the right color for him."

Owen waved her off before sighing and looking down at his soda. He twirled the straw around in the drink for a moment before he tensed. Lukas felt his own body stiffen. Seeing Owen freeze made him nervous.

Lukas raised his eyes and looked around, trying to center in on whatever made Owen tense. His eyes darted from table to table, eventually trailing to the windows. A young man in a dark red hoodie with a large tear on the arm stood outside across the small parking lot of the diner smoking.

Goosebumps prickled across his skin as a cold terror ran through his body.

"Archer, he's back," Lukas whispered, grabbing Archer's sleeve as he leaned over the counter.

"Weird, he didn't order anything today on the phone," Archer mumbled, flipping through an order pad.

"No, Archer, that's the guy that–!" Lukas panicked, suddenly feeling heat start to replace the fear he had felt moments earlier.

Archer inhaled sharply. "Lukas, you need to get back to Owen and stay with him. Now."

Lukas felt scorching fire running through his veins as he realized what was about to happen. He stood, trying to get back to the booth where Owen sat, but he suddenly tensed up as every scent in the diner became ten times stronger. Then, shocks ran through his body, as if a bolt of lightning had just struck him.

He froze, balancing his weight on the back of a nearby chair. Owen rushed over to the frozen omega, steadying him with his own body. Lukas looked up, trying to keep his eyes on the stranger, finding that Owen was doing the same. He whimpered when he saw that the stranger had extinguished his cigarette and was walking toward the front entrance of the diner.

"Archer, we have to go. Now," Owen whispered.

Archer nodded. "I know, go out the back!"

At his side, Lukas trembled, and Owen's attention immediately shot to him. Lukas simply turned his head and buried it in Owen's side, breathing raggedly. Within a moment, Archer was directing Owen, Lukas, and Sienna into the breakroom. He gave Sienna a knowing look and began walking over to the front door. Owen's arm tightened around Lukas' waist, half-carrying, half-dragging the omega to safety.

Sienna locked the breakroom door behind them, walked over to Archer's desk, and pulled out a set of keys.

"You can get to your car out the back door while Archer keeps him occupied. Pretty sure that guy won't be back after Archer gets hold of him. Still, I would stay away from the diner for a few days just in case." Sienna disabled the back door's alarm and opened it for Lukas and Owen.

Nodding, Owen pulled Lukas closer to his side and walked through the doorway. "Thanks, Sienna. Be careful of that guy."

"You don't have to worry about me, tough guy. Archer takes care of his employees," Sienna smiled and gave a thumbs up. "Now, get him home, okay?"

Lukas was looking worse and worse by the second. He could feel his body heat searing through their clothing. Sienna locked the door behind them as the two men walked to their car.

The ride home was silent. Lukas could practically feel Owen's blood pressure rising by the minute. The alpha growled roughly as Lukas groaned in the seat next to him.

Owen gripped the steering wheel tighter. "Are you okay?"

Shivering, Lukas curled up in the seat as much as the seatbelt would allow. "Well, this isn't good."

Owen's body tensed up at the sound of Lukas whimpering. "We'll get you settled at home as soon as possible, and then I'll go out and pick up some medicine and snacks for you. Okay?"

When Lukas didn't answer, he heard Owen shift, cocking his head toward the omega.

Lukas' mind was racing. He curled his arms around himself, happy when Owen didn't push the question.

Within a few minutes, they stood outside Lukas' home. Owen carefully led him inside to the bedroom and eased him down onto the bed.

"I'll be back in a few minutes. Any particular snacks you want?" Owen questioned, keys and wallet in hand.

A few moments passed before Lukas finally spoke.

"I think it would be best if I just rest by myself for a few days. I can't ask you to… I can't cause any more trouble for you," Lukas whispered.

"You're no trouble, Lukas," Owen protested.

Lukas bit his lip, groaning quietly.

Owen was quiet for a moment. Finally, he spoke up, "Lukas, are you sure? Will you be okay by yourself?"

I can't ask for his help.

"Listen, I'll leave you alone if that's what you want, but I'm still going to go out and make sure you have plenty of snacks and medicine," Owen whispered.

But it hurts. It's so hot. I'm scared.

Lukas moved from a sitting position to lie on his side, facing Owen. The alpha ran his hand through Lukas' hair before moving down to cup the side of his face. His thumb massaged small circles on Lukas' reddening cheek.

He's done so much already.

"If you decide you need someone to talk to, I'm just a phone call away. I'll call to check on you every day if you want me to," Owen calmly said, breathing deeply before he walked to the door. "Just take care of yourself."

I'll get through this. Don't worry, Owen.

That's what he wanted to say, but only a shuddered sigh escaped his lips as he watched Owen stand in the doorway.

Owen sighed, looking over Lukas with concern before standing and leaving the bedroom and closing the door behind him.

Lukas gritted his teeth, finally letting out a bit of the pain he was feeling now that Owen couldn't see him.

I've gotta try. I am a McGuire. I've been through worse than this. I can beat this.

CHAPTER 7

*L*ukas heard his alpha's car start up and listened as the noise disappeared into the city. He rolled over onto his back and curled his fingers into his hair, pulling lightly as if to snap himself out of his trance.

"Not my alpha, damn it. Not my alpha!"

He moaned quietly as the thought of the redhead crossed his mind. He had seen the way Owen's muscles tensed with each sound he made, and he knew just how much of an effort it must have been for the alpha to leave him behind.

Lukas heard a muffled meow from the closed door. It took all his energy to rise from the bed and open the bedroom door. As expected, there sat Miss Mulberry, angry that Lukas had dared to go to bed without feeding her.

Slowly shuffling down the stairs, Lukas carefully stepped around the cat that was weaving in and out of his legs and eventually made it to the kitchen. After filling the creature's food dish, he made his way back upstairs and closed the bedroom door again.

"Sorry, my little Mulberry. This is gonna be a rough one. Can't have you in here tonight," he whispered to the small creature who was still in the kitchen. He knew he'd hear her protesting at the closed door later.

Lukas' vision spun as he turned around to walk back to the bed. He grabbed his dresser for support and tried to balance himself.

His breath came in ragged pants as the room finally stopped spinning. His entire body pulsed with heated energy.

"Ah, hell."

He tried to calm himself, cursing the way his body was reacting to every little turn and touch.

"Just gotta sleep this off. Can't ask Owen to take care of me again," he murmured, regaining his posture. He dug in the dresser and picked out the comfiest pair of clothes he owned.

Closing the drawer, he made his way to the bathroom, dragging his hand across the wall for support. The cold tile of the bathroom floor chilled his feet. Balancing his weight on the sink with one hand, he opened the medicine cabinet and took out a small bottle of sleeping medication.

Lukas popped the cap off and took a dose before cupping his hands and gathering some water from the sink. He splashed the cold water on his face, sighing as the water trickled down his neck and back.

He dressed, opting just for boxer shorts at the last minute, and dragged his body out to the bedroom. He managed to draw the curtains of one of the windows closed before collapsing on his bed.

Despite being so warm moments before, a chill suddenly danced across his skin. He wrapped himself in a quilt, and, a spasm ran through his body. He brought his legs closer to his abdomen as a spark coiled in his stomach and buried his face into his pillow before a quiet whimper escaped his lips.

· · ·

Darkness flooded his vision. Try as he might, he couldn't see anything, but he could feel rough lips on his neck and a strong arm pinning his wrists above his head. A low, possessive growl reached his ears. He felt a calloused hand running down his thighs, pushing his legs up. He struggled at first, his heart rate picking up until he heard a calm, charming voice laced with desire. That voice sounded so familiar–

Lukas jolted awake, sitting up. It was one in the morning, and he was covered in sweat. Moonlight was streaming in through the parted curtains, giving his bedroom an ethereal glow.

Lukas fell back onto his pillow, a shameless moan slipping from his lips.

"Oh, fuck," Lukas whimpered, panting quietly as pleasure pulsed through his hips.

He felt as if the very fires of Hell were dancing about his room. He reached to throw the quilt off and was shocked by a pain in his lower body. He sat up in discomfort.

"Oh, my God, am I thirteen again?" Lukas hissed, leaning his head back on the pillow and staring at the ceiling.

Lukas turned onto his side and hid his face in his pillow. He remembered the touches from his dream. They ghosted across his skin, causing an unbearable heat to well up inside him.

He felt his hand moving on its own as he closed his eyes tightly and remembered more of his dream. It drifted lower past the elastic band of his boxers until it reached its target. He wrapped his hand around his member, and a ragged gasp escaped his lips.

He bit down on his bottom lip slightly, his body

curling forward as he began stroking in a gentle rhythm. He remembered the sparks he'd felt when Owen had touched him. Those rough hands caressing his face. Those strong arms holding him close and protecting him in his time of need. That low growl in the diner when someone threatened them.

He imagined what it would be like to feel Owen's weight on him. A comforting, protective weight surrounding him, driving deep into him as his legs wrapped around the alpha.

Lukas' hips jolted forward, a spasm running up his spine. He carefully shifted his legs, letting his boxers slip further down.

Chills danced across his exposed skin before he turned to lay on his back. Fluid leaked from the head of his dick as he gripped it in his hot hand. He threw an arm over his eyes and his mouth hung open as he panted, picking up the rhythm as he thrusted up into his hand.

He wondered how it would feel to completely expose his back to Owen as he hid his face in embarrassment, gripping the pillow in front of him, trying to silence his moans before–

A low whine hit his ears as the obscene sounds of his slick flesh filled the room.

–before Owen would snake an arm around his chest, pulling him up from the bed, pulling him flush to his warm chest. Owen would carefully tilt his omega's head to the side, exposing the flesh of his mate's neck, ready to stake his claim.

One final bite on his neck, enough to draw blood, would seal the pact. The act would bind them together physically for a short while, but the claiming bite would be forever.

Lukas' legs trembled as he got closer to the edge.

Owen would be powerful, ultimately making him lose all semblance of thought as their instincts took over. He would be filled entirely, plowed into the sheets as he moaned *his* alpha's name.

"Oh, fuck." His voice drawled out long and slows he thought of all the filthy things *his* alpha could do to him.

He gripped the edge of his pillow, lost in pleasure before he saw white. He threw his head back and gasped, his toes curling as he came, white ribbons shooting back onto his stomach and bed.

Lukas' body twitched and spasmed as he rode out the aftermath, slowly coming down from his high. He opened his eyes and stared at the moon-white ceiling.

The spent omega cringed, feeling something slick running down his legs. He felt sweaty, dirty, and empty, but most of all…

Lukas turned his head and looked at the cold, empty side of his bed.

Lonely. He was alone. Lying in that spacious nest of soft blankets and pillows, only when he thought of Owen did he feel at peace. He needed the alpha here.

When he could finally move, he carefully sat on the edge of his bed before standing, dragging his hand across the wall to get to his dresser.

Lukas quickly found a pair of loose sweatpants before picking up his cell phone. As he dialed Owen's number and heard the first ring, his knees buckled, and he fell forward, his phone clattering somewhere on the dresser.

Lukas whimpered softly. His hands gripped the edge of the dresser as pleasure ran up his spine. He felt the familiar heat welling up in his stomach.

Lukas heard someone's breath hitch before asking, "Lukas?"

Owen's voice startled him for a moment. He had been so lost in pleasure that he hadn't heard the alpha answer the phone.

His entire body felt so hot. He tenderly held the phone to his ear, sinking down to the floor to sit on his knees. He rested his forehead against the cool wood and brass handles of the drawers in front of him, shuddering at the difference in temperature.

"You heard that? Well, that's... embarrassing," Lukas whimpered quietly.

He heard Owen shift over the phone and growl.

"What do you need, Lukas? I'll help however I can." A faint purr rumbled through the speaker. "Tell me what you need, *omega*."

Lukas shifted his legs and quivered. His free hand gradually shifted down. It took every ounce of strength for him to stop himself from slipping his hand past his waistband again.

"F-fuck." His body trembled, ragged breaths leaking from his lips.

"Lukas." Owen's concerned voice echoed through his ears.

He whimpered into the phone and heard Owen draw in a sharp breath. Here he was. This was him. A wanton omega kneeling on the floor, wanting nothing more than to be close to his alpha – to be happy, loved, and *full*.

Lukas swallowed his pride and took the leap.

"I need you here, Owen. I need you, *alpha*," he gasped into the phone.

A faint rumble reached his ears before Owen said in a reassuring tone, "I'll be there soon. I promise."

Lukas looked sullenly at the phone as the screen indicated Owen had ended the call. Not being able to hear Owen's husky voice left him empty once more. He pulled himself off the dresser before walking over to his armchair, peeling open the curtains, and cracking the window.

Curling up in his chair, he willed himself to doze for a few minutes, breathing in the early morning scents. It was much different than back home. There, he would always catch a scent of rain on the wind and sometimes, the smell of the livestock down in the barn. Here, he smelled many different foods, car exhaust, and…

A sour scent suddenly hit his senses. An alpha's scent. A disturbing mix of desire and dread frisked across his body.

"That can't be Owen," he hissed, crinkling his nose.

Gathering his courage, he pulled himself from his chair and peeked out the window at the street. A shadow stood near his home, looking around cautiously before walking up onto his small porch.

Losing sight of the figure, he quickly closed the window before he was startled by a loud bang on the front door.

"Definitely not Owen," Lukas whispered to himself. Another bang hit the front door.

Lukas hobbled as quickly as he could to the bedroom door, putting all his strength into moving his dresser to block the entrance.

Getting the dresser into place, he saw his phone lying on the edge. He grabbed it and ran for the bathroom, locking the door and looking around for something to brace it with.

His eyes landed on the hamper full of dirty clothing.

"Well, hot damn, maybe my dirty laundry will actually be of some use," he joked with himself, trying to calm down. If anything, it would buy him some time until Owen arrived.

Bracing the heavy hamper underneath the doorknob, he reached into the towel closet. He dragged out some towels to pile around the bottom of the basket and stuff under the door.

Satisfied with his hasty fortifications, he stepped back. He redialed Owen's number before dragging a dirty collared shirt out of his hamper and throwing it on.

He heard a final bang at the front door and then silence. The familiar creaks on the steps told him all he needed to know. Turning off the bathroom light, he popped the thick collar of his shirt over his neck, buttoned it shut, and listened for Owen's voice.

The phone rang twice before Owen picked up. Distant car horns echoed through the speaker.

"Sorry, I was trying to avoid a couple of dumbass drivers. Are you okay? Do you need me to pick up anything on the way?"

"Owen, someone's here. They're–"

Lukas whimpered in fear as there was a bang on the bedroom door. His panicked breaths reached Owen's ears as they both heard the intruder grunt with each hit.

He heard Owen's car accelerate before the alpha's low voice whispered, "I'm almost there. Stay hidden."

Lukas heard the scrape of the dresser on the hardwood floor as the stranger pushed the door open. He wedged himself in the towel closet and closed the shuttered door.

His ears perked up at the sound of drawers opening, followed by the closet door in his bedroom. The stranger was rifling through his room without a care in the world. Lukas' scent was strong in the bedroom, especially after his recent romps, this much he knew. Maybe that would keep the stranger busy for a while.

The sound of the bed frame creaking faintly hit his ears. He heard a low growl and the rustling of the sheets and pillows.

A ragged voice drifted throughout the room, "Where are you, my sweet omega?" Lukas heard the sheets rustle once more and then a sharp intake of breath.

He clenched his legs as a quiet, shuddered moan slipped from his lips. He shifted in the small closet space before a spasm ran up his spine, and his eyes blurred. He slapped his hand over his mouth. The bitter scent was all he could focus on, no matter how terrible it was. *Alpha. Alpha.* It repeated over and over in his mind, his body pulsing with every echo.

The noise from his bedroom stopped, and a cold feeling of terror rushed through his body. The silence dragged on for a few moments before heavy footsteps echoed through the small bedroom.

The sudden slam against the bathroom door startled Lukas into letting out a short yelp. His heart pounded in his ears as the stranger continued bashing the door before it finally gave way.

Lukas heard his hamper clatter to the floor and listened to the heavy breathing of the stranger as he crossed the threshold. He heard the squeak of the door, and the light flicked on, revealing a huge shadow outside the shuttered door.

There weren't many places to hide in here. He knew he would be found quickly. Lukas carefully moved and wrapped his hand around the closest object, and not a moment too soon.

The closet door slowly opened with a creak as the stranger stood looking down at the omega hidden in the darkness.

"Well, hello there, cupcake," came a familiar voice.

Fire ran through Lukas' veins as he heard the voice.

The man's hand came toward him, trying to drag him out of the closet. Despite having nowhere to go, Lukas instinctively shrank back into the closet, trying to get further under the shelves. He swung his arm out, hitting the man with whatever he had picked up.

The alpha growled before dragging Lukas from the closet, his weapon clattering to the cold tile floor.

Anger rolled off the alpha. He dropped Lukas to the ground and turned and leaned against the locked door, staring down at the omega and blocking any means of escape.

Lukas lay on his stomach. He lifted himself up onto his elbows before raising his head and seeing the familiar men's boots. The smell of cigarette smoke mixed with the bitter scent hit him. It suddenly made sense.

"So, it was you that night." Lukas' voice wavered before he dragged himself to his knees, leaned back against the bathtub, and looked up at the man's face. A recognizable dark hoodie with a large gash in the arm covered his body, and a bandanna covered everything but his suddenly familiar, amber eyes.

The man's eyes flashed before he lowered the bandanna. A raving smile crossed his face. He crossed his arms and looked down at Lukas before introducing himself.

An unfitting game show announcer's voice drawled from the alpha's mouth. "Hi, Lukas. Aaaaaaron Hudson here. I'm sure you remember me."

Aaron put a hand over his heart. As his smile grew wider, his eyes grew fiercer. "I think I played the part of the unassuming beta pretty well, don't you?"

Fear washed over Lukas' face.

"You may have forgotten me, but you didn't forget my touch. I saw the fear in your eyes when I grabbed your wrist at the diner. You tried to hide it, but I saw." Aaron sighed.

Lukas groaned as he shuddered. Aaron's scent was terrible. He wanted Owen.

"You know, I waited every day for your response to my letters. Visited you in the diner a lot. Hell, even used scent blockers so I could get to know you better without you being scared of me."

Aaron buried his face in his hands, sighing.

"And then I see you hanging off the arm of another alpha. I watched as your striking eyes only saw *him* and not me…"

Lukas looked up at the delirious alpha. Those eyes bore deep into his soul, demanding answers.

"You even went out of your way to talk to me, to take care of me when…" Aaron sighed, looking down at his bandaged fingers. Lukas' eyes trailed up to the gash in the alpha's hoodie.

"Yeah. Remember this?" Aaron asked, carefully pulling up the sleeve to his elbow. Lukas cringed when he saw stitches crisscrossing the gnarly-looking wound. "Pretty cool, right? Had to do it myself. If I had gone to a hospital, they would have asked questions."

"It doesn't look cool; it looks infected! You need to get it treated properly." Lukas' voice wavered. He saw mixed emotions in the alpha's eyes.

"And here you go again. Do you treat everyone this way when they're hurt? Or only me? Do you take care of that other alpha like this? Or is he too good to get injured?"

Aaron growled, pulling the sleeve of his hoodie down again.

"Listen, what happened in the diner, it might have been something small and insignificant to you, but to me, it was everything. I could finally look you in the eyes and talk to you and take in your scent and..."

Aaron's voice trailed off, followed by a frustrated, heated groan.

"All this time, I've wanted only you. I tried to get your attention, but you were always surrounded by people. Fun, creative, quirky people I could never compare with. I thought the letters were my only chance to be noticed. I wanted to take it slow and easy, give you a chance to know me as I want to know you, but catching your scent that night in the alley, then in the diner, and especially tonight..." Aaron's voice lowered.

"...it's driving me wild." A feral growl escaped the alpha.

It was at that moment, looking into those crazed eyes, that Lukas knew there was no reasoning with this man. Mr. Yorke's words echoed back in his mind. *No. I'm not going to be a victim. Not this omega.*

He had to stall for time. Just until Owen got there. He thought back to the effect his voice had had on Owen when he called the alpha earlier.

He shifted his emotion into one of submission, dipping his head and bowing forward to put his hands on the tiled floor between his slightly parted knees. His fingers curled at the chill.

Putting on his best helpless voice, he whispered, "I'm sorry, alpha," breaking eye contact with the larger man, looking off to the side.

Aaron growled under his breath, stepping away from the door and crouching in front of Lukas. His bitter scent changed a bit, indicating that Lukas was doing the right thing.

Lukas looked up with sad eyes. He forced himself

to think of sad memories so he could cry, further proving his need to apologize to the angry alpha. He let his mouth hang open somewhat, letting small breaths leak from his lips.

"I'm sorry to have caused you so much pain," he whimpered before lowering his head again, cocking it slightly to "inadvertently" expose a bit of his neck.

Lukas heard Aaron's low growl again. He felt the alpha get closer, his breath sour and hot. Aaron's hands ran over his thighs. Just a bit more.

The alpha purred, "Good. *My omega.*"

"I truly am sorry," Lukas apologized one last time, allowing a whine to escape his throat as he felt Aaron pull him from his kneeling position.

Suddenly Lukas was wrenching the tension rod from the wall above him. He put all his strength behind the rod as he hit the crouched alpha on the side of his head, the shower curtain falling to cover the man.

Aaron fell to the floor in pain, clutching his head before rage filled his eyes.

That cold stare froze Lukas in place for a moment before he snapped out of it and hobbled out of the bathroom. He slammed the door behind him and threw his armchair in front of it.

Try as he might, Aaron had wedged the dresser in such a way that he couldn't move it in time. The angry alpha broke out of the bathroom, holding his head. He focused on Lukas as he stepped forward.

"No more running, *my little omega,*" Aaron hissed.

CHAPTER 8

$\mathcal{L}$ukas scrambled back, trying to get away from the enraged alpha. The man had blood trickling down the side of his face, yet he still persisted.

"What are you so afraid of, my little omega?" Aaron asked quietly, advancing upon the retreating figure.

Infuriated by Lukas' silence, a roar thundered from the injured man.

"I'll take care of you better than any other alpha! So, what are you so afraid of!?" Aaron yelled louder.

Lukas stepped back until his hips hit his nightstand. He looked back and replied with a smile, "Why, I'm simply afraid our time together will slip away!"

With that, Lukas chucked his heavy alarm clock at Aaron, hitting the alpha in the abdomen, knocking the wind out of him.

"You should wake up and smell the roses, my friend!" Lukas picked up a vase of flowers and flung it at the winded figure, causing him to fall to the floor.

"And you know what else?" Lukas asked.

A snarl came from deep within the alpha.

"You really should see the light at the end of this tunnel. I hear it's a beautiful sight!" Lukas threw his old lamp at the kneeling figure. *Damn, I'm gonna miss that lamp.*

Lukas looked back at his nightstand, searching for anything else to throw, but he found nothing. He tried to throw Aaron to the side to put some distance between him and the enraged alpha before he was dragged back. He felt his stomach hit his mattress before the alpha's weight fell against him. His arms were pulled back and held behind his hips.

Aaron ran his free hand across Lukas' exposed skin. He traced his fingers around Lukas' jawline, careful to avoid getting too close to his mouth.

"Bit the hell out of me last time. Won't make that mistake again," Aaron whispered, crowding himself closer to Lukas.

Lukas squirmed under his touch, trying to push himself back off the bed. He felt weak, like his muscles were made of taffy, and his struggles were ineffective against Aaron.

"You know, I could almost mistake you for an alpha with your fighting spirit. Only thing that gives you away is that sweet, *please-fuck-me* scent of yours."

A scared whimper slipped out of Lukas' lips as he turned his head away.

"Don't struggle. I'll take care of you, I promise," Aaron said.

"You're not Owen, so you're not..." Lukas turned as far as he could to look at Aaron over his shoulder, trembling.

"I'm not who? Say his name again. I dare you," Aaron threatened.

A moment of silence passed between the two.

Aaron, content with the silence, sighed roughly, forcing Lukas to flip over.

"I'll make you feel better than he ever could. Ain't man enough to take what he so clearly wants," Aaron growled.

Running his hands over Lukas' hips and legs, he paused as he heard the omega begin to growl.

"Now what are you doing, my little omega? Speak up." Aaron carefully strained his ears to hear, ducking his head down to listen.

Lukas let out one last groan, feeling Aaron let his guard down before hissing, "...You're. Not. My. Alpha."

With one last surge of strength, Lukas butted his head forward suddenly, hitting Aaron square in the nose. At that moment, the dresser blocking the door was shoved to the side, and the weight forcing him against the bed was gone. He slumped to the floor and saw that he was in the protective shadow of Owen, who was squaring off against Aaron.

Owen's lips were drawn back in a snarl. His eyes were burning with a cold vengeance that sent a shudder through Lukas' body.

"Should have known it was you," Owen growled. "Couldn't leave well enough alone, huh?"

Aaron chuckled, shrugging.

"Why are you so upset? He's not yours. He's not anybody's! But you haven't known him nearly as long as I have. You can't possibly love him like I do," he snarled at Owen with cold eyes.

Owen looked around at the carnage in the room.

"You have a damn twisted definition of love."

Turning back to look at Lukas on the floor, Owen snarled.

"Now, here's the deal. You're either going to roll

over like a good little defeated alpha and surrender before the cops get here."

Aaron smirked. "Or?"

Owen cracked his knuckles. "Or you're going to put up a decent fight before the cops get here and *then* roll over and surrender. Your choice."

"You're not alpha enough for him. He'll be mine by the end of the night," Aaron growled before launching himself at Owen.

Owen redirected Aaron's momentum with ease, throwing him into a wall on the opposite side of the room. He threw a knowing look over his shoulder at Lukas, sliding his cell phone to the omega before Aaron threw himself at him again.

This time, Owen caught Aaron's fist in his and kneed him in the stomach, throwing him to the floor.

"Come on, you little bastard, I said a decent fight!" Owen's voice thundered, yelling at the alpha on the floor. Lukas felt his pulse pounding in his head as he quickly shuffled back against the wall and called the police.

Aaron went low, knocking Owen off his feet. After receiving a couple of solid hits, Owen quickly set his legs in a firm position and kicked the rival alpha off him, launching him across the room and against the wall. A few framed pictures fell to the hardwood floor, sending glass across it.

Stunned, Aaron wheezed as he tried to stand, but Owen's fist connected with his face before he could recover. Owen quickly threw his rival to the ground and dug his knee into his torso, his arm at the rival alpha's throat.

Owen bared his fangs at the alpha beneath him. He was seething with such anger that the room was suffocating. Owen began to place more pressure on his arm as Aaron struggled to breathe.

"Yield!" Owen snarled at the rival alpha. Lukas shuddered as that word slipped from his alpha's mouth. A small voice nagged at the back of his mind, getting louder with each passing second.

Submit to him. Bare yourself to him. Touch him.

The losing alpha tried to pry Owen's arm off his throat, kicking his legs in a fury, but eventually held his hands up in submission, gasping as air filled his lungs again.

Owen quickly flipped Aaron over, binding his arms and legs with some clothing that had been strewn around the room during Aaron's search, before looking over at Lukas. The omega was leaning against the side of the bed, arms wrapped around himself, taking in shuddered breaths.

"You're okay now, Lukas. You did good," Owen crooned from across the room, hoping to comfort Lukas. He couldn't risk leaving Aaron unattended to hold the shivering omega.

Lukas groaned as Owen's scent strengthened, blocking out the bitter odor of Aaron.

Victorious alpha. A qualified mate. Vigorous alpha. Virile alpha. Hold me, mark me, make me yours.

Lukas quietly moaned in response, trying to banish the feverish thoughts racing through his mind. His own sweet scent started filling the room, and he heard Aaron squirm and snarl beneath him, trying to tear at his binds.

"Listen, I'm not a bad guy, I'm just an alpha who wants to take care of him!"

Owen growled, forcing Aaron's head down to the floor. "Let me let you in on a little secret. It may come as a shock to you, but a true alpha is one that guides, protects, and provides. Underneath that tough exterior, they love their mates deeply..."

Owen's voice lowered, "...but they never, *ever*, force their urges on *anyone.*"

"And have you been a *true alpha?*" Aaron retorted sarcastically.

"I strive to be one every day. The world doesn't need any more alphas like you," Owen snarled. His gaze softened as he glanced at Lukas.

The police were at Lukas' home within a few minutes. Neighbors were attempting to see what was happening, but many were turned away by the police. A voice stood out from the crowd as someone hustled inside the bedroom.

"Lukas? What the hell happened here?" Came a feminine voice.

Lukas weakly looked up at the source.

"Sienna?" Lukas looked surprised to see her there.

"You big doof, are you okay? What about you, Owen? What happened?" Sienna rushed over to her friend, looking him over before looking toward the alpha.

"It was Aaron," Owen growled, cracking his knuckles.

Sienna's mouth hung open in shock. "No way, why would he? Is he...?"

"Yeah. Alpha. Had his eyes on Lukas for a while and snapped when he saw us together. He tried to..." Owen's voice trailed off. He bristled with anger as he looked at Lukas crumpled on the floor.

"Oh, that sick bastard," Sienna fumed with anger. "Lukas?"

Sienna sighed, sitting on her knees next to Lukas.

"It's pretty bad, isn't it?" she asked cautiously, slowly placing her cool hand to his hot forehead. He shuddered at the contact.

"I just feel empty." Lukas' voice was hoarse, whispering so only Sienna could hear.

Sienna looked up at Owen, pleading with her eyes. Owen nodded.

"Lukas, I know exactly what you're going through, and I know you're scared, but you need to stick with Owen, okay?" Sienna said in a forceful tone. "I've got to get back to Hazel. She got really scared with all the ruckus going on. If you need me, I'm staying with my parents tonight. Be safe, honey."

Owen and Sienna followed the remaining police to the front door, listening as the sound of their cruisers slowly died away in the noise of the city.

"You know what this means, right? Sienna asked Owen.

"Yeah, I do. I can't believe he's–" Owen buried his face in his hands, sighing. "He's mine, and I'm fated to be his. I mean, I knew after we finally met outside the bar, but you're never truly prepared to meet your fated. And then it just happens."

Sienna smiled. "You better take good care of him."

Owen tensed, face flushing for a moment before he turned to the woman. "I will. I promise."

"Here, take this. I don't have a cell phone, so if you need me, call this number." Sienna handed over a small piece of paper with something written on it.

"Oh, this must be–" Owen took the paper, flipping it in his hand to read the contents.

"Yeah, my parent's number. I'm staying with them for a couple of nights since Mom recently had surgery. If I don't answer, their names are Andre and Dahlia."

Owen nodded, "Thanks, Sienna. Try not to worry about us. I'll get him to safety, and you should get back to your little girl and parents."

"Take care of him, okay? I know how painful that kind of heat can be," Sienna whispered, gazing back up the stairs before stepping out onto the porch.

Shutting the door and locking it, Owen quickly turned to climb the creaky stairs and almost slipped on something. He looked down and saw some faded, crumpled papers that looked very familiar. Archer had had them at some point.

Concern flooded him as he saw exactly what the papers were. He gripped them tightly as he walked back into the bedroom. Lukas was still in the same spot next to the bed, groaning softly. His eyes lit up with desire as he saw Owen enter the room.

Owen slowly walked over to kneel in front of Lukas, moving the omega's shaggy hair out of his face.

Lukas leaned into his touch as he looked around his destroyed room. He looked up at Owen, lifting his hand to carefully examine the cuts and bruises on the alpha's cheek.

"We should really get you cleaned up. Those look painful," Lukas whispered.

Owen took Lukas' hands in his and kissed them lightly, whispering, "Nah, it's nothing. A sucker punch. I've had worse from the bars in Vegas."

Owen's lips left his hands, and he pulled Lukas close. The omega went lax against the warm body in front of him, and he took in Owen's scent deeply. Feeling the caresses of the alpha, Lukas felt warmth drift across his body.

A low whine escaped Lukas' lips.

Owen sighed before whispering, "You're going to stay with me until this passes. I'm not letting you out of my sight again. We're gonna pack up some clothes for you, we're gonna pack up Miss Mulberry, and we're gonna stay in my apartment tonight."

The sound of Lukas' shuddered breaths filled the room. Owen ran his hand through Lukas' hair and exhaled slowly before showing the worn papers to Lukas.

"This is how he found you. Remember these?" Owen passed the packet to Lukas.

"The fair plans I lost. Son of a–" Lukas cringed. "And there's my address. Yeah, Mr. Yorke was going to send someone to pick up the baked goods for the fair directly from here." Lukas groaned before ripping up the papers and throwing them to the side.

"I need your okay on this, Lukas. I'm not going to kidnap you, hurt you, or do anything you don't want. But I can't leave you alone in this destroyed house. It's not safe," Owen anxiously added, looking at the shattered glass and overturned furniture scattered around the room.

Lukas nodded slowly, using his nightstand as support to try to stand before falling again. Owen helped Lukas onto his bed, checking him for wounds before laying him down.

"I'll throw a suitcase together for you. Does Miss Mulberry have a carrier anywhere?" Owen asked.

"Hallway closet. She has a favorite blanket and bird toy down on the couch, too. Food is in the pantry, bottom shelf." Lukas threw his arm across his forehead as he stared up at the ceiling.

"Okay. I'll be back in a jiffy. Try to get some rest," Owen rushed off to gather everything, switching off the light as he left. Lukas turned his head to stare out the window and saw that clouds had gathered in the past hour, dimming the moonlight.

Lukas sighed. He really didn't want to be alone right now, but he knew Owen couldn't be in two places at once. Didn't make it any easier, though.

"Just for a little while, you'll be fine," Lukas whispered to himself.

The curtains remained open, the longing for

privacy forgotten in the midst of the attack. As time passed, the clouds cleared slightly, letting moonlight reflect off the shattered glass on the floor.

Lukas felt a nostalgic feeling bloom in his chest. The scattered glass painted an illusion of stars on the ceiling above his bed. Ignoring the gnawing heat in his body, he marveled at the sight with a tired smile until his eyes grew heavy.

The squeal of the brakes roused Lukas from his sleep. Owen's scent was all around him. Opening his eyes, he realized he was in Owen's car.

He heard Miss Mulberry meowing in her carrier in the back seat.

"Hey, sunshine. We're already here." Owen threaded his fingers through Lukas' and squeezed lightly.

It was still dark outside. The clock in the car indicated it was just past two-thirty.

"Let's get you inside and settled, and then, maybe, we can get some quality sleep," Owen whispered to the drowsy omega.

Undoing his seatbelt, Owen stepped out of the car and came around to the passenger side. He gingerly raised the seat up and helped Lukas stand before placing the omega's arm around his neck and sweeping his arm under his legs.

Lukas squirmed as he grabbed the alpha's shirt, shocked to suddenly not be on the ground. A few moments passed, and he relaxed, leaning into Owen's chest.

Lukas groaned, torn between fighting sleep and

doing something about the heat gnawing away in his stomach. He leaned his head back to look up at the sky before the tin awning of the apartment building blocked his view. He caught a familiar scent before it was blocked by the city again.

"...'s gonna rain tonight," Lukas whispered, slurring his words together.

Owen looked up at the sky. There were only a few stray clouds illumintated by the moon against the dark sky.

"How can you tell?" Owen questioned.

A small chuckle slipped from Lukas' mouth. "Can't mistake that smell. Rain on the wind."

Lukas nuzzled back into Owen's neck, smiling.

Slowly working his way up the stairs to his apartment, Owen felt his body shudder at the contact. He pulled Lukas tightly to him before arriving at his door.

Quickly unlocking his door, he stepped forward, carefully maneuvering Lukas' head and legs through. Within a moment, they were greeted by a giant fuzzy creature.

Owen tiredly glanced down at the dog, smiling before saying, "Well, hello, O' Guardian of the Den. Lick anyone to death while we were gone?"

Mimosa bounced around happily, sniffing Owen's legs as he walked past before returning to her bed next to the couch.

Owen's apartment was small, but it was cozy. It was painted in darker, more moody colors that made the apartment cave-like. Dark curtains blocked out the streetlights and dampened the noise from the streets below. A simple lamp in the corner dimly lit the entryway and living room.

Books and newspapers were scattered about the coffee table, and small succulents dotted the windowsill above Mimosa's bed. Framed pictures of various city skylines lined the walls above the couch and down the hallway.

Owen made his way down the hallway and carefully nudged open his bedroom door. The room was a bit messy, but it would do for now. He slowly made his way across his room, careful to avoid any of Mimosa's squeaky toys. No need to summon the beast.

His full-size bed was pushed against the wall in the far corner just below one of the windows. It was covered in pillows and blankets arranged against the headboard and under the window.

The curtains were drawn open, and the blinds were a mess. Mimosa had probably been in here looking out the one window she could reach. The tattered blinds allowed the pale yellow light of the streetlights to creep across the bed.

Owen pulled back the old fleece blanket, helping Lukas under it, before surrounding the omega with more blankets and pillows.

"I know the last thing you want is to be covered in heavy blankets, but it'll help soothe you for a bit while I'm gone. I'm going to run back down to get Miss Mulberry. I've set up a small place for her in the other room until she gets introduced to Mimosa. I'll be back soon, I promise," Owen whispered, running his hand through Lukas' shaggy hair.

Lukas nodded, sinking into the warm nest and wrapping up in the blankets. Despite the sweat that covered his body, it was oddly comforting. Owen shut the door as he left, fearing Mimosa would come in and harass the recovering omega.

Lukas heard the front door close as he stared up at the ceiling with half-lidded eyes. He took a deep breath as he relaxed into the soft bed, and an intoxicating fragrance overwhelmed his senses.

A needy mewl leaked from Lukas' lips as he turned and buried his nose in the source. He felt the tension leaving his body, replaced by a considerable need as he took in Owen's scent. He felt a jolt of desire shoot through his body, straight to his hips.

Grabbing a pillow and taking in the heady smell, he slowly started grinding down into the mattress. Surrounded by the warm pillows and blankets covered in his alpha's scent, the soft grinding motion sent shivers down his body. His mouth hung open in a silent plea for more, eliciting a quiet groan.

A door in the hallway loudly squeaked open, shocking him out of his trance. He shot up out of the bed, falling onto the floor with a hard thump before he heard footsteps rushing to the bedroom.

"Lukas?" Owen's voice reached his ears. He scooted against the bed and tried to stand as the bedroom door swung open, failing to get to his feet in time. He shut his eyes so he wouldn't have to see the worried alpha, if only for a few moments.

With his back against the cascade of blankets, Lukas pulled his knees to his chest, laying his head back against the plush blankets, exposing his throat. Ragged pants escaped his lips.

Owen's calm voice was suddenly next to him. He hadn't heard the alpha stride across the room. "Are you okay, Lukas?"

He knew Owen could smell his arousal, see the bulge in his sweatpants. He felt dirty, getting so turned on by the alpha's scent, and at the same time, it felt so right.

Lukas was quiet for a moment before replying in a shuddering breath, "I'm burning up, empt–" Lukas' voice suddenly caught in his throat as a spasm ran through his body.

"'s too much," Lukas slurred.

Shivering, Lukas averted his face, focusing on the side of the room away from Owen. Out of habit, he reached up to pull the brim of his hat down, flinching when he realized his hat was still at his house.

Lukas covered his face with his hands and sighed, trying to will away the immense load of embarrassment he was feeling.

Owen crouched in front of Lukas, slowly taking the omega's hands in his. Half-lidded, teary green eyes stared back at him, framed by a face hot and flushed red with shame. Each breath they took warmed the small space between them.

Owen pulled Lukas into a hug, leaning forward slightly to whisper in his ear, "Please don't try to hide from me, Lukas, I–"

Lukas whimpered as Owen sighed, blowing hot breath in his ear.

"I know you're scared right now. A lot of shit has happened tonight. But I don't want you to be afraid of me, too. It would kill me," Owen whispered.

Lukas squeezed Owen's hands before he doubled forward with a whimper, his toes curling in his shoes as another jolt ran through his body. Owen sat on his knees, shifting closer to the omega.

"Why… would I be afraid of you?" Lukas asked.

"Because every fiber of my being has changed. Before I met you, I was always alone. The quiet was unsettling, close to unbearable. Now, I know you. Whenever we're together, I'm happy. When that bastard broke into your home and tried to hurt you, when he touched you, I was infuriated. I'm happy I was able to protect you, but if what I did scared you, I'd never forgive myself." Owen's head dipped down onto Lukas' shoulder, thinking about what had happened.

A moment of silence passed before Lukas whispered, "'s how do you feel now?"

Owen tensed up, lifting his head to look Lukas in the eyes before saying, "I want to protect you. I want to make you laugh, make you feel better, show you new and exciting things, but most of all…"

He lowly growled his last sentence, licking his lips, "…*I want to make you mine.*"

Lukas' grip tightened as he curled his fingers into Owen's thin t-shirt. The alpha pulled Lukas to his feet.

Lukas felt one of the alpha's large hands resting on the curve of his lower back and the other cupping the side of his face. Owen leaned forward.

"I just need to know you want this, that you want me as much as I want you," Owen said in a breathy voice next to Lukas' ear.

Owen finally released Lukas from the embrace, gazing into his dazed green eyes.

Lukas shivered. A deep, desperate longing flooded his body.

A pleading whisper leaked from the omega's mouth, "Owen, I want you. I want to be yours."

A warm purr rumbled deep in the alpha's chest.

"As you wish, my omega."

Owen's gaze lingered on Lukas before his arms wrapped him in a protective embrace. He slowly began to lean forward, sealing the pair in a kiss.

Hearing a low purr, Lukas slowly parted his lips, exhaling heated whimpers as Owen deepened the kiss. As if the whimpers energized Owen, he pressed forward with a sudden intensity, causing the pair to fall back into the soft bed.

Within a moment, Lukas' back was against the

pillows near the headboard. He invited Owen closer, resting his legs on either side of the other man's waist.

Lukas' hands softly threaded through Owen's hair, drawing him into a heated kiss, breaking only to throw their shirts across the room.

Owen's hands wandered from Lukas' face down his back to his hips. He pulled Lukas' hips up as he scooted closer, closing the gap between them, grinding lightly before returning his hands to the omega's face.

Cupping Lukas' face, he gently pressed kisses to his forehead, then his cheeks, before claiming his lips once more. Owen's movements were slow, longing, as if he was adoring a beautiful piece of art.

Owen threaded his hand through Lukas' hair, slightly pulling the omega's head back to expose his throat. The alpha's tongue slowly dragged across Lukas' throat, nipping here and there at the exposed flesh.

Owen's hands ran down the nape of Lukas' neck slowly, lightly scratching down his back and sides An obscene moan escaped Lukas' lips as Owen bucked his hips forward hard.

The sound made Owen growl before his hands slipped past the waistband of Lukas' sweatpants. The alpha backed his hips off a bit, hearing a needy whimper from Lukas as the warmth of his hips vanished.

Owen bent forward, careful not to drag his hips against Lukas' again. He kissed the omega's face as he teased and toyed with his body, ever-so-slightly rubbing Lukas' dick through his boxers. The rough movements forced more sweet, heated sounds to escape Lukas' lips as he tried to hide his face against Owen's neck.

Growling, Owen quickly removed their remaining clothes, Lukas' scent mingling with his own. Owen felt the omega's legs slowly wrap around his hips, forcing them close together.

Owen wrapped his hand around Lukas' stiff flesh, stroking the omega up and down. Sweet moans escaped Lukas' mouth, hot against the alpha's shoulder. Owen felt Lukas' fingers dig into his back, curling in pleasure.

Slowly moving his hands downward, Owen purred when his fingers felt slick. Lukas threw his hand over his mouth, biting his lower lip lightly as he tried to block out the sounds he was making.

"*I want to hear you,*" Owen whispered.

Lukas' pleading eyes met Owen's before he slowly removed his hand. At that moment, Owen smirked and hooked his fingers into Lukas, causing the omega to cry out in a mix of shock and pleasure.

"*Stunning,*" Owen purred low, his eyes fixed on Lukas.

Lukas' hips bucked up before they were forced down with a strong arm.

"*Just relax. Let me take care of you,*" Owen groaned quietly.

Lukas closed his eyes as he gave in to the pleasure. His euphoric moans filled the room as Owen moved his fingers in and out of him. Soon, he felt empty once more.

Opening his eyes, he looked up at Owen, his desirous gaze meeting the alphas. In Owen's eyes, there was a feral look, desperate, loving. It was enough to make Lukas turn his head and close his eyes, unable to withstand the steamy gaze.

"*Lukas.*"

He heard his name being whispered over the pounding of his own heart.

"I need you." Owen let out a growl, nipping at and kissing Lukas' neck. He spoke softly, his words only intended for his omega's ears.

A bolt of pleasure shot through Lukas' abdomen.

"Please take care of me, alpha," Lukas whispered, wrapping his arms around Owen's neck.

Within a moment, Lukas felt an enormous pressure as Owen's cock started to fill him. He threw his head back in a moan. The alpha's heated voice next to his ear and the feeling of finally being filled made his entire body tremble.

Owen began moving with a slow, steady roll of his hips before picking up the pace. The room was filled with the lewd sound of flesh hitting flesh. Lukas was lost in the new sensations, listening to the low moans of his alpha before he felt himself being lifted up off the bed.

Suddenly, his knees were on either side of the alpha's, and he felt himself sinking down onto Owen's cock. Lukas moaned and arched his back against Owen's waiting arms, the alpha's hands tracing lines down Lukas' back.

"Beautiful," Owen purred as he ran his tongue across Lukas' chest, planting kisses across the flesh before lying back against a pile of pillows.

Lukas' pleading gaze met the alpha's. He was embarrassed at this new position. A deep red hue covered his face as he placed his hands on Owen's shoulders to balance himself.

Owen carefully placed one hand on Lukas' hip, gripping it roughly. His other hand ran slowly up Lukas' arm, and he threaded their fingers together once the alpha reached his omega's hand.

He looked Lukas up and down before smiling, his eyes full of passion. He pulled the omega's hips down as he suddenly thrust up into him, causing

Lukas' body to jolt as a blissful moan leaked from his lips.

"Do you feel it? How deep I am inside you?" Owen groaned as he felt Lukas' clench around him.

A small chuckle slipped from the alpha's lips. *"That made you tighten up. Damn, so you're into dirty talk, hmm?"*

Lukas' eyes were half-lidded, staring down at the alpha beneath him. His mouth hung open, panting.

Owen's warm gaze met his omega's as a smile graced his lips. His hands gripped Lukas' hips as he drove him down onto his cock.

"I'm going to love on you until you can't think. I'll mark you and make you mine."

Owen slowly rolled his hips up into Lukas at a maddeningly slow speed.

"I'll take it nice and slow, waiting until you least expect it, and then–"

Owen quickly settled back into a rhythm, thrusting up into the omega bouncing on his lap. He pulled Lukas flush to his chest. His fingers danced down Lukas' spine, flitting here and there as he reveled in the small whimpers and moans. He looked up at his moaning mess of an omega, letting his hands travel down to Lukas' hips, forcing them down hard.

Lukas whimpered, lowering his head onto Owen's chest.

"Let it all out, sweetheart. I'm gonna fill you to the brim," Owen purred, his hips bucking as he felt his omega tighten up at his words.

Pleasure shot through Lukas' body as he arched his back. He rested his hands on Owen's legs as he bounced to meet Owen's thrusts.

"I'm gonna fill you up, stretch you out, make your body tremble in pleasure."

Owen quickly sat up and wrapped his arms around Lukas, one hand threading into the soft hair at the nape of his neck, the other tracing lines up and down his back.

"Gonna plant my seed in you, make you swell."

Owen growled as he buried his face against the curve of Lukas' neck. He pulled back, looking into the eyes of his omega, looking for any hint of uncertainty as they grew closer to their limits. Lukas gazed back into those blue eyes and moaned, exposing his neck further.

Lukas saw white as he reached his limit. White seed shot in thin ribbons across their stomachs as he felt Owen throb deep within him. He closed his eyes as he felt a sharp pain on the curve of his shoulder and neck, followed by the silky feeling of Owen's tongue. At the same time, he was filled with a warm, wet heat from the inside, Owen's cock deliciously stretching him.

"Mine. My beautiful omega."

Owen's muffled whisper reached his ears. In a daze, he opened his eyes, planting slow kisses across his alpha's face.

Lukas smiled against his alpha's skin, drawing Owen's face up with his hands before kissing him once more. He felt Owen's arms curl around him protectively, and sighed into the kiss.

Lukas felt his body cooling off before his eyes grew heavy. He locked his ankles behind Owen's back and wrapped his arms around the alpha's neck, leaning forward to take in his scent.

Soft pillows framed his body as he felt himself being moved onto his side. A warm blanket was pulled up to their hips, and Owen pulled Lukas closer.

"Rest, sweetheart. You're safe here. I'll take care of

everything, just get some sleep," Owen whispered in a husky voice.

The room was dark and quiet save for their slowly relaxing breaths and Lukas' whimpers whenever Owen shifted.

Thunder rumbled in the distance, followed by the patter of rain against the window. Owen carefully raised his free arm to reach over Lukas and twist open the blinds slightly. He watched the rain fall through the small slits in the blinds, running his hand through Lukas' hair idly, expecting to hear the soft snores of his omega soon.

"I love you," came a faint whisper from his side.

Owen jumped, just a bit, at the sound of the voice. He froze before his chest suddenly burst with warmth as if he had just been given a gift he had wished for his entire life.

"And I love you too, Lukas."

CHAPTER 10

*L*ukas' eyes slowly fluttered open. He remembered a sweet dream, warm blankets, and soft pillows. Miss Mulberry was on the windowsill looking outside at the birds. He didn't hear the noises of the city any longer. Instead, he heard cows?

Sitting up in bed, he realized he was in his old room. He would recognize those tacky posters anywhere. The scent of cooking food thoroughly roused him. Standing, he walked the path he had so often walked before, stepping around the cat weaving between his legs instead of stepping around scattered toys.

Rounding the corner into the kitchen, he beheld quite a sight. There stood Owen cooking a huge breakfast. Mimosa sat faithfully by his side, hoping a bit of meat would fall to the floor.

"Morning, beautiful. You were out like a light. Figured you might appreciate a good breakfast when you finally emerged from the cave." Owen smiled.

As Lukas drew closer to investigate the skillet full of food, Owen pulled the omega into his arms and kissed him.

Lukas smiled into the kiss as he felt Owen's hands on his hips. Breaking away, Lukas looked around the kitchen.

Strewn throughout the living room and kitchen were streamers, balloons, and party games. A small pile of gifts sat on the counter.

"You should get ready. Our guests will be here soon."

Lukas looked puzzled. "Guests?"

At that moment, a knock resounded on the door. Owen carefully put his spatula to the side and swung the door open, calling out a greeting with a smile as he took a step back.

Lukas' jaw dropped as he felt his eyes burning. His Ma and Pa were crowding the doorway, smiling and happy. Well, it was official. This was his favorite dream.

Lukas dove into their arms, hugging them tightly as the tears finally fell.

His Ma's voice hit his ears first. "Oh, why are you crying, dear? It's a wonderful day for a get-together." A bright smile decorated her face.

A hearty chuckle boomed through the living room. His Pa stepped forward and ruffled Lukas' hair.

"Nice jammies, boy! C'mon, it's been too long. Let's enjoy a nice breakfast."

The dream shifted, and the next vision put him at the table surrounded by his family. Breakfast had been finished, and Lukas watched as everyone laughed and joked. He smiled as Owen reached over and threaded their fingers together.

Suddenly, a soft cry came from upstairs. Lukas jumped at the sound, worried that Miss Mulberry might have gotten caught in something.

"I'll get her. She's probably ready to start this

party." Owen smiled, then stood and walked up the stairs.

Confusion filled Lukas' mind. *Surely not.* His Ma's voice jolted him from his thoughts.

"You've chosen a good mate, sweetie. You two have built such a wonderful life together. We couldn't be happier for you," she whispered.

"Another generation of McGuires. It just gives me the fuzzies. Though I guess she would be an Atkins. Ah, well, she has McGuire blood in her veins." His Pa chuckled.

"And you named her after your dear mother." His Pa smiled. "It suits her. A beautiful name for a beautiful girl."

At that moment, Owen came down the stairs with a toddler in his arms. She looked like a little doll. So many emotions filled Lukas as he saw his mate holding her. She was dressed in a pink footie pajama set, and her dark red hair was a complete mess. Her bright green eyes were darting about, gazing at all the people in front of her.

"There's the girl of the hour! Happy birthday to my favorite granddaughter!" His Pa's voice boomed across the kitchen and the little girl giggled.

"Three years old. Where did the time go?" His Ma smiled, taking the little girl from Owen and bouncing her on her leg.

"Speaking of where... where did Pa go?" Lukas looked around the living room, shocked that he hadn't heard his Pa get up and leave the table. He swore that man was secretly a ninja.

As if on cue, his Pa carried a large tray of cake pops over to the kitchen table.

"I think the little one wants some cake," he said.

Owen snickered.

"I think you just want some cake, pops." Owen

looked over at Lukas, sporting a dumb smile on his face.

"Noooo." Lukas held his head in his hands.

Lukas' dad laughed. "You caught me red-handed."

The little girl giggled, squirming on her grandmother's lap as her family began to sing happy birthday.

LUKAS TOOK IN A DEEP BREATH. THE SKY WAS SLOWLY turning pink and purple as the sun set. His little girl had worn herself out playing with her new toys and had been put down for a nap. He heard the livestock in the fields as he was sitting on the front porch with his mother while his dad and Owen watched some goofy comedy movie on TV.

His mother's voice cut through the silence.

"I really couldn't be happier for you, sweetpea." She relaxed in her rocking chair. Miss Mulberry sat on her lap, purring happily.

"I'm so happy with him, Ma. I don't know how I got so lucky," Lukas whispered, staring off into the sunset.

"Fated mates are hard to find, but when you finally find each other, it's like something out of a fairy tale." she smiled, watching Mimosa run around in the front yard.

Lukas thought for a moment, sighing.

"I wish this could last forever, Ma. All of us together, enjoying days like this, but I know..."

"I know, honey. I'm sorry we can't stay longer, but we have to get back. Your father has work tomorrow, and I have about five loads of laundry to do. He's always so filthy when he gets home between his volunteer work and the work on the farm." His mother laughed.

Lukas felt his heart wrench into pieces as his voice cut off with a choked sound. Yeah, he knew the truth, but he was content to live this dream just a bit longer.

The dream started fading away bit by bit as the sun set. His Ma stood from the rocking chair and placed Miss Mulberry on the porch railing as his Pa came out onto the front porch.

"Well, I think it's about time for us to head out. It's getting a bit late." His Pa stretched his arms high above his head.

Lukas quickly dragged his parents in for a long hug.

"I love you, Ma. Love you, Pa," he whispered as tears started falling.

Owen stepped out onto the porch, setting a tin of leftovers down on the swing before wrapping his arms around the group.

"You've done well, boy." Lukas' Pa shook hands with Owen. "Most young alphas don't know how to treat their mates, but I want you to know that I trust you wholeheartedly with my son. You better look out for him and that little girl of yours, or I'll haunt you forever. Deal?"

Owen laughed. "Deal, sir."

"It's time, Lukas. You all be safe. Be happy. Be sure to eat well and take care of each other, okay?" Lukas' Ma smiled, taking Owen and Lukas' hands and placing them together.

"And give your brother a call sometime. I'm sure he misses you," his Pa said as he took his wife's hand in his.

The sun started getting lower and lower as bits and pieces of the dream faded away. As darkness covered the farm, everything began vanishing, until the light reached the edge of the old farmhouse.

"Time to wake up, Lukas. We love you." His Ma whispered. He felt her hand caress his cheek as his vision faded.

WHEN LUKAS OPENED HIS EYES, THE LIGHT OF THE streetlights was gone. He felt warm arms wrapped around him, holding him close. Snores filled the room as he propped himself up on his elbow to look over Owen's sleeping form at the clock on the nightstand.

"Six-thirty," Lukas sighed to himself, easing back down onto the mattress.

Owen snorted in his sleep, slowly cracking open his eyes.

"You okay, babe?" Owen murmured.

Lukas thought for a moment, examining his arms and stomach. His body didn't feel like it was about to burst into flames anymore, but he was very sore. He felt the faint sting of scratches and bites all over his neck and back.

"You've been crying. Was I too rough?" Owen asked, lifting his hand to run his thumb across Lukas' cheek.

Lukas' own hand shot up to his face, feeling the remnants of the dried trails on his cheek. He bundled up close to Owen before whispering, "I had a dream about my parents. I was able to hug them and talk to them and… it's like they were actually there."

He felt Owen's lips on his forehead as his arms drew Lukas close.

"Wanna talk 'bout it?" Owen's words were slurred with fatigue, but he kept his eyes focused on Lukas.

Lukas shook his head.

"Not right now. Get some more rest. We can talk about it later."

Owen purred, carefully watching Lukas before his eyes started to drift shut.

Lukas sighed, and he heard Owen's snores not long after. He turned over onto his side, facing the window. The curtains had been drawn shut, blocking out most of the light and noise. Only a sliver of light came through across the bedspread. He closed his eyes, thinking back to his dream, as he began drifting off.

Miss Mulberry meowed outside the closed bedroom door, making Lukas jump.

Mimosa soon started whining as well, and Owen sighed, carefully pulling his arm out from under Lukas and the pillows. As he sat up, the blanket rolled down to his hips. He stretched his arms high above his head, muscles flexing tantalizingly. Lukas' eyes followed the alpha's arms until–

A snicker inadvertently slipped out, causing Owen's gaze to drift to the omega buried beneath the covers.

"What?" Owen asked hoarsely. Fatigue still dripped in his voice.

"Your hair. It's a complete mess." Lukas giggled, sitting up and fluffing the dark red mayhem.

Owen waited until Lukas shifted a bit closer before his arms suddenly wrapped around him again. They fell back, Owen pulling Lukas down against his body for a hug before flipping him over and pinning the omega to the bed.

Owen peppered kisses on any exposed flesh he came across, freezing when he reached Lukas' neck. He took in a deep breath, shuddering slightly before sighing.

"My beautiful omega."

Lukas mewled against the alpha as another whine was heard outside the door.

Owen sighed, pressing one last kiss to Lukas' lips before sitting up.

"C'mon, sweetheart. We gotta take care of the kids." Owen chuckled.

LUKAS FELT A COLD BALL OF DREAD SETTLE INTO HIS stomach as he stood outside the front door to his home. It seemed that some of his neighbors had patched up the door, but he could still see boot marks from Aaron's assault. Mimosa bumped against his leg and Miss Mulberry's carrier, whining. He felt Owen's hand on his lower back as he shuddered.

"Are you sure about this? We can give it a couple more days if you want," Owen said, concern lacing his voice.

"The faster this is all cleaned up and washed away, the better." Lukas sighed.

Swallowing his fear, he took his key out and pushed open the door. The sight that greeted him was hard to see. Aaron had really done a number on the entryway. He carefully set the carrier down in the living room before returning.

His shoes had been scattered across the entryway and hall, and there were water stains on the hardwood. Nearby, an antique vase he had had forever was destroyed, the fresh flowers he had bought from Sawyer's shop wilted among the pieces. Most of the framed family photos he had hanging in the stairwell were shattered on the floor of the entryway and stairs, left behind in the darkness of the invaded house.

Owen, holding tightly to Mimosa's leash, watched as Lukas climbed a few of the steps, sturdy boots crunching on the small bits of glass. Carefully brushing away the shards, Lukas picked up the old family portrait Owen had seen on the first day he visited.

Lukas sighed, stepping back down to Owen before showing the picture to him.

"I was twelve when we took this picture. It was our last photo as a family," he whispered.

Tracing the face of the man in the photo, Lukas began to speak quietly.

"So this is my Pa, Thomas McGuire. He was one of the hardest workers I've ever known, but he always had time to spend with his family. He always put on a tough front, but he was a big softy inside and a huge fan of puns. You two would have definitely gotten along."

Owen chuckled to himself as he looked at the man in the photo. He had bright green eyes, dark brown hair, and a tall, built frame with tanned skin. In the photo, he was stooping down to kiss a woman on the cheek while at the same time giving bunny ears to a small boy in front of him.

Lukas' finger moved to a short woman in a yellow gingham dress who had wild, blonde locks hidden under a wide straw hat. She had fair skin, brown eyes, and an infectious smile. She was laughing as the photo was taken, no doubt from the surprise kiss.

"And my Ma, Abigail. Toughest woman I've ever known. Everyone around town always said she didn't have a mean bone in her body, but she knew how to strike fear into my heart when I needed it." Lukas shuddered.

Owen tightened his arm around Lukas' waist, pressing a small kiss into the omega's hair before looking back down at the photo.

"And, by God, she was one hell of a cook. Ma loved feeding everyone when our town had events. You should have seen her baking up a storm whenever fall rolled around." Lukas' voice trailed off with a smile.

"Pa would open up our farm to the public for corn mazes, bonfires, and hayrides as soon as it started getting cool enough, and she'd bake for days. My brother and I weren't allowed in the kitchen much in the fall since we tried to sneak bites of some of the treats." Lukas chuckled at the happy memory.

"Naughty. Though, if she was as good a cook as you are, I don't blame you," Owen whispered with a smile.

"And there's my partner in crime, Colton." Lukas pointed to the taller of the two boys standing in front of their mother. He had his mother's blond hair and brown eyes. He was practically screaming teenage angst but still smiling at the antics going on behind him.

"I haven't talked to him since I left. I get the feeling he's angry with me, like he feels I wasn't happy with the work he did to provide for both of us after Ma and Pa passed away," Lukas said sadly.

"Won't know until you try, babe. Don't assume. That's the biggest mistake you can make." Owen lightly squeezed Lukas' waist.

Lukas relaxed into Owen's arm for a moment before wiggling from the grasp, bending to pick up another photo.

"And here's Miss Mulberry, all fluffy after her first bath. Should have seen her before I got this picture. I thought she was a black cat when I first brought her home." Lukas giggled, grabbing another photo.

"A picture of the old farm. You know, my great-grandfather built that house from the ground up. Always loved that huge kitchen with its view of the fields." Lukas gazed toward the small kitchen in his home before picking up one last photo.

"And then our last family fishing trip. Colton caught the biggest catfish I'd ever seen that day." Lukas got a dreamy look in his eyes. "We stayed at the lake until dark, watching the sun set and the stars appearing as we grilled that sucker."

Owen saw Lukas' shoulders slump with a sigh as he held the pictures and looked around at the mess.

"And we haven't even gone upstairs yet." Lukas gazed up the stairwell.

Owen stepped forward, about to say something, before he heard a noise in the doorway behind him.

A hoarse voice called out, "Lukas? That you, boy?"

CHAPTER 11

"$\mathcal{K}$nock knock, neighbor," a woman's rough voice said through the doorway.

At the sound of the voices, Lukas poked his head around Owen's body to see who was at his door. An older African-American man stood there, holding his arm out for his wife, who was balancing her weight between his arm and a cane.

At the sight of the two people, Lukas' eyes lit up.

"Andre, Dahlia! Oh, Dahlia, is it okay for you to be out and about like this so soon after your surgery?"

Lukas made a motion to invite the couple inside, leading them past the carnage and into the living room. Andre slowly helped lower Dahlia onto the couch as Owen led Mimosa past the glass shards to sit in the living room.

"Why, I'm fit as a fiddle, darlin'. Don't let this worrywart make you think otherwise. I'm more worried about you, to be honest. Sienna told us about what happened, and poor Hazel has been worried sick about you since you weren't home last night." Dahlia's eyes shifted between Lukas and Owen.

Lukas took Owen's hand in his, shifting closer to the alpha.

"Yeah, if not for Owen here, it would have been a lot worse." Lukas shuddered, burying one side of his face against the alpha's warm shoulder.

Andre stood from the couch, shaking Owen's free hand.

"Good on ya, boy. Thank you for protecting Lukas from that piece of shi–"

Dahlia shot a look at her husband, cutting off his sentence.

Andre flinched, clearing his throat. "I mean… that piece of crap."

Dahlia nodded, smiling at Owen before her gaze drifted to Lukas.

"And I do have to thank you for those meals you sent. Lord knows I love this man to death, but our kitchen would be burnt to cinders if I left him alone in there," Dahlia cackled and Andre looked sheepish.

"It's the truth. I consider myself lucky that I have been blessed with a wonderful wife who is a master in the ways of the skillet." Andre put his hand over his heart and bowed to Dahlia, smiling.

"Ah, stand down, you old gollumpus. You already get three square meals a day. Don't have to suck up to me anymore," Dahlia snickered, kissing Andre's cheek. "And I meant to tell you, Lukas, Sienna and Hazel are gonna be stopping by too. We're all gonna help you clean up, and we're not gonna take no for an answer."

Before Lukas could say anything, a little girl's voice pierced the room.

"Lukas? Are you home!?"

"Told you. Can't say no because they're already here." Dahlia grinned impishly.

"Hazel, be careful of the glass!" Sienna's concerned voice boomed from the hallway.

Lukas chuckled before a flash of purple and pink

ran through the living room and jumped into his arms, knocking him back into Owen's chest. Owen instinctively wrapped his arms around Lukas and the newcomer, steadying them so they wouldn't fall.

"Oh, critical hit!" Lukas groaned as the little girl in his arms laughed.

Sienna came around the corner and giggled at the sight.

"Hazel, sweetie, you gotta be a bit more careful with him. He had a rough night last night." Sienna glanced over Lukas' shoulder.

The little girl looked a bit guilty and climbed down before looking up at Owen in confusion.

"Well, look at you, Hazel. Is that a new dress?" Lukas asked, crouching down to the girl's level.

"Yep, Eliseo made it for me. Isn't it pretty?"

The girl twirled around with a smile, flaring out the pleated skirt and showing off the matching shorts and gold bracelet.

Lukas gasped, smiling at the little fashionista.

"Absolutely beautiful. Eliseo really outdid himself this time."

Sienna made a noise of agreement from the corner of the entryway, smoothing down the back of the dress as Hazel stopped twirling.

"He's very talented. I'm surprised he hasn't opened his own shop yet. I'm sure he would do very well."

"Actually, he's planning on setting up a booth at the Heated Hullabaloo, so maybe that will get his name out there," Lukas replied, standing up and intertwining his fingers with Owen's.

The girl escaped her mother's hold and looked positively shocked at the person who was holding hands with her friend. She looked the alpha dead in the eye, probably studying him for any weaknesses before grinning from ear to ear.

"You're new. What's your name?" she asked. "I'm Hazel. Hazel Adgate."

"Well, hello, little princess. I'm Owen. It's a pleasure to meet you." Owen smiled, crouching down to Hazel's level.

"He's my knight in shining armor, Hazel, so you better be nice to him." Lukas ruffled the girl's hair, earning a giggle.

"You have pictures on your arms. Did you draw those yourself?" the girl questioned, spying Owen's tattoos.

Owen opened his mouth to respond but didn't get to utter a word before Hazel continued on her roll.

"And these marks. Mama said those are called scars?" Hazel looked over to her mom, and the woman nodded. "Yeah, scars! Did you get them protecting Lukas from scary things? What did you save him from? Was it big? Was it–"

Sienna scooped up the girl mid-sentence, earning a squeal.

"Hazel, calm down, sweetie. One question at a time. Why don't you go check on Papaw and Mammy? They should still be in the living room."

Hazel ran to her grandparents and Miss Mulberry as Sienna walked over to Lukas and Owen.

"So, you seem like you're feeling a lot better, Lukas."

Sienna winked as Owen pulled Lukas close in a side hug, kissing his hair.

"Yeah, Owen took good care of me." A dark flush decorated Lukas' cheeks as he spoke.

Sienna let out a small sigh, crossing her arms, before smiling.

"Yeah, judging by that mark, you won't ever have to worry about going through your heats alone again."

Lukas' hand shot up to his neck, fingers trailing the bite mark, before ducking his head.

A quiet snicker slipped from Sienna's mouth as Hazel came back over to the group.

"Hey, are you going to come to my birthday party, Lukas? And you're invited now too, Mr. Owen, because Lukas really seems to like you, so you must be a good person!"

Lukas reeled. He had almost forgotten about the little girl's upcoming birthday with everything that had been going on.

Crouching down to the little girl's level, Lukas smiled brightly, disguising his moment of forgetfulness.

"Of course, Hazel. I wouldn't miss your party for the world! Tell me what kind of cake do you want this year?"

"Strawberry! With bright pink icing and lots of sprinkles! It's gonna be a mermaid party, so there's gonna be lots of seashells and water, and I'm gonna be the mermaid princess!" Hazel trembled with happiness.

Suddenly, she froze, eyes locked on the crook of Lukas' shoulder.

"Are you okay? What's wrong with your shoulder? Do we need to go to the doctor?" Hazel asked, cocking her head.

Sienna stepped in, putting her hand on Hazel's back and steering her to the hallway before Lukas could answer.

"Oookay, it's clean up time! Who's ready to clean!?"

"But Mama, what if Lukas needs to go to the

doctor? We can take him to that one we went to when I was sick. She was really nice."

"Lukas is fine, sweetie. Trust me. This is just something that eventually happens to every omega."

"Even you, mama?"

"Even me, sweetpea." Sienna carefully pulled back her blouse, exposing the faded scar on the crook of her shoulder, showing the young girl her mark.

Sienna reached into the closet and grabbed a small broom and dustpan, ready to sweep up all the glass on the floor.

Andre stepped into the hallway, saying, "Hazel, sweetpea, can you please go check on Mammy? I'm going to help with the cleaning down here, and she may get lonely sitting all by herself on that couch."

"Okay, Papaw." The little girl scampered off as Lukas and Owen filed into the hallway.

"I almost forgot about her party. I'm such a horrible adoptive uncle," Lukas lamented, whispering to Sienna.

"Don't worry about it, Lukas. You've been through a lot in the past week. And I know you volunteered to bake a lot of stuff for the fair, so if you're not up to baking her cake this year, I can make something. Don't strain yourself, you doof," Sienna whispered.

"I'll help with anything I can," Owen suddenly chimed in. "After all, we're a team now."

Andre chuckled nearby. "Yeah, I guess you are. Can't say no to a face like that, Lukas."

Lukas looked at Owen's face and was shocked to see his alpha giving him puppy eyes.

"You're right, how can I refuse?" Lukas grinned, wrapping his arms around Owen. "All right. Now, let's get to cleaning. We have a lot to get done."

· · ·

As the sun began to set over Boston, the house was filled with the comforting scent of hearty food and baked goods. Lukas wiped the sweat from his forehead and let out a sigh, opening the small window in his kitchen to help cool the room down.

He leaned against the windowsill to rest for a moment, listening to all the people moving around in his house, each and every one chatting and joking. It reminded him of the holidays when he was younger.

Over the course of the day, a few neighbors had come and gone, helping out and spreading goodwill. It was a real sense of community that Lukas hadn't been expecting. He focused on plating the food he had been slaving over for the past two hours, setting up the table as a little thank you for his friends and neighbors.

He was so caught up in his plating that he almost didn't notice a small hand creep over the side of the counter, reaching for a homemade doughnut.

"And just who dares to steal the treasure of Doughboro?" Lukas asked in a menacing voice, peeking over the counter. He expected to see Hazel, but he had to hold back a laugh when he saw Archer crouched on the floor next to her, looking guilty. Just when did he sneak in?

"Quick, our cover has been blown, H-2935! Abort, abort!" Archer yelled as he picked up Hazel and ran for the living room. Lukas noticed, too late, that the girl had grabbed three of the doughnuts from the plate, giggling the entire time.

"Ye shall be cursed! A monumental sugar high ye shall have!" Lukas yelled after the pair, laughing as he returned to setting the table. He began to think about the events of the day when it hit him. A full house, good food, good company, lots of shenanigans. He was seeing his dream again, only this time, he was awake. He was sure of it.

A voice startled him from his thoughts. Owen had stepped into the kitchen and wrapped his arms around Lukas from behind. As he rested his head on the omega's shoulder, he sighed.

"Long day. Gonna sleep like a rock tonight," Owen whispered.

Lukas snickered.

"You can't sleep yet. I have to fatten you up first." Lukas motioned to the meal set out on the table. "Go wash up. Spread the word that it is time for sustenance."

"Yes, sir." Owen smiled, pressing a kiss to Lukas' cheek before unwinding his arms and heading upstairs.

Smiling to himself, he looked back over the small, worn book lying open on the counter. It was his mom's old recipe binder, filled with every recipe he had loved growing up. He flipped carefully through the pages, fingers trailing across the doodles she had drawn.

The sound of approaching voices and laughter prompted him to close the binder, and he placed it on a nearby bookshelf before everyone seated themselves at his small dining table. It was almost comical seeing so many people trying to cram themselves around such a small table, but nobody seemed to mind.

As Lukas sat at the table, the world around him seemed to fade out. His gaze shifted to Owen, who was sitting across the table between Hazel and Andre. His alpha looked so handsome with that goofy smile, and his laugh was infectious. He was a presence that filled the entire room. Lukas could practically feel the cartoon heart pounding out of his chest, and he wouldn't have had it any other way.

CHAPTER 12

"Can't believe I let myself be talked into this. Haven't been to a bar in ages," Sienna muttered under her breath, hiding a smile.

"Come on, even moms have to unwind, girl! Take a load off. Your parents have Hazel for the evening, and I won't be drinking, so you two can go wild if you want," Archer clapped a hand on the woman's shoulder, talking over the music and chatter of the bar.

Lukas was nervous about being back in the bar. Though the warm glow of the stained glass lights above the tables was inviting, he looked about warily. He didn't feel any eyes on him like last time, and if someone did look his way, they quickly became disinterested. He idly ran his hand over the healing bite mark on the crook of his shoulder.

Archer pushed Lukas forward toward a table near the bar, waiting to catch sight of the redheaded alpha. "Just have a drink and enjoy yourselves. My treat."

"You sure we won't be bothering him?"

"Lukas, let me let you in on a little secret." Archer threw his arm across Lukas' shoulders, sighing dramatically. "Owen adores you, and I know if I had a partner that I absolutely adored, I would love to see them whether we were at work, in town, at home, or wherever."

Sienna removed her jacket and draped it over the back of her chair. A waitress dropped off three menus and took drink orders before rushing off to other tables.

"Yeah, don't worry so much, Lukas. Just have a drink and relax."

Lukas trembled slightly. "Easier said than done."

Sighing, Sienna laced her fingers together and placed her hands on the table.

"Lukas, think about that mark on your shoulder. If anyone comes over here to try anything, they will become the very definition of stupidity, especially since Owen's scent is heavy around here."

"Well, speak of the devil," Archer mumbled.

Lukas followed Archer's eyes to the door to the kitchen. Owen was approaching the bar, his steps hurried.

"Oh, come on! Let's move over to the barstools. We'll sneak attack him," Sienna whispered excitedly, dragging Lukas along.

"You kids have fun. I'll just stay back here and be the guardian of the coats," Archer called after them, leaning back in his chair and looking over the menu.

Climbing up onto a couple of free barstools, Lukas and Sienna watched as Owen gathered many glasses and bartender tools, ready to put on a show of skill. He hadn't noticed the pair at the end of the bar yet, and with an act of flair, he began juggling bottles and glasses effortlessly.

Lukas watched the show with awe. Every time it seemed like a bottle was going to crash to the floor, Owen was there to snatch it midair before sending it on its way again. This way and that way, low and high, the bottles went on a magnificent trip before reaching their destinations. Glasses rolled along his arms before they were tossed behind his back, ending up balanced on his shoulders before they were back in the air. They finally made a safe landing on the bar to be filled with perfect shots.

Every person witnessing this amazing feat of wizardry was starstruck. Mr. Yorke stood nearby, arms crossed and smiling, clearly proud of his apprentice. The man carefully snuck over to Owen, whispering something in his ear before motioning toward where Lukas and Sienna were sitting.

Owen finally noticed Lukas, and his eyes lit up. Lukas turned to his left and was about to smile at Sienna, but he found himself grinning like an idiot at an empty barstool. He spun around and looked back at the table where the traitor was sitting, giving him a thumbs up with a smile.

Lukas turned around just in time to come face to face with Owen. The alpha planted a chaste kiss on Lukas' cheek before taking his hands.

"Babe, I'm so glad you're here! Did you see? I thought for sure I was going to mess that up, but everyone seemed to love it!"

"I couldn't believe what I was seeing. You were incredible! Guess all that training in Vegas is gonna make you a big star here," Lukas said.

Looking back to where Owen had been standing, he noticed that Mr. Yorke had taken over bar duty. When he noticed Lukas staring at him, he motioned to Owen with a smile and nodded at Lukas.

Owen stretched, groaning a bit.

"That means it's break time. I would say we could go over and sit with Archer and Sienna, but…"

One gaze over to the table showed that Archer and Sienna had found a few old friends. They were chattering quietly, sharing drinks, appetizers, and mindless banter.

Owen reached behind him and took a bottle of Lukas' favorite drink down from the shelf, showing it to Mr. Yorke before grabbing a glass and walking out from behind the bar.

"That's fine, though. Means we can hang out in the quiet of the breakroom. I know how tense you are being back here, and I know you don't like crowds like this."

Wrapping his arm around Lukas' waist, Owen led him back to the cozy room. Sitting down on a familiar couch, Lukas noticed that Mimosa's bed in the corner was distinctly lacking said lump of golden fur.

"Mimosa is still at the apartment. I couldn't roll her out of bed today. Really, I couldn't. Miss Mulberry was sleeping on top of Mimosa." Owen chuckled, setting the bottle and glass down on the low table in front of the couch. "Think it's safe to say they get along well."

Pouring a small glass for Lukas, Owen wrapped his arm around the omega, leaning into his warm body with a contented sigh.

"You know, it wasn't my plan. Becoming a bartender. It just sort of happened."

"Like everything else on this crazy ride of life, right?" Lukas hummed, downing the drink in one go. He winced as the burning liquid hit his tongue, shuddering as he felt the warmth settle in his stomach. "So, how did you end up in the business?"

Owen made a small sound in the back of his throat, and silence filled the room. His arm squeezed Lukas a little bit tighter.

"My dad was a drunk. A mean one. That's why everyone was so surprised when I went into the bartending business. I figured if I could learn more about the trade, I could teach others and help them be more responsible with their indulgences."

Lukas snaked his arms around Owen's form, leaning into him.

"Thankfully, he didn't stick around long, but it was tough," Owen continued.

Lukas furrowed his brow. He'd always hated seeing people drunk and disorderly back home and was always thankful that those close to him never walked down that path.

"Mr. Yorke was actually the one who trained me before I left for Vegas. If not for him, I wouldn't have lasted a day in those bars. He's been more of a father to me than that stumbling asshat ever was."

Owen leaned back on the couch, smiling up at the ceiling in a daze, no doubt reliving the good memories he had of growing up around Mr. Yorke.

"What about your mom?"

"Cripes, Mom. She was lucky. Dad ran off pretty quickly, but I know it wasn't easy on her being a single mom. She moved in with a friend of hers who lived in Norwood after I left for Vegas. She was always rough around the edges, but she was good to me and did her best to spoil me once in a while."

"Would it be possible for me to meet her?"

"Yeah, absolutely! Not sure when her schedule will allow her time to come up, but I'll give her a call soon."

"It's okay. We have all the time in the world. I'm not going anywhere," Lukas whispered, cuddling into Owen's side.

A comfortable silence filled the room as Lukas' eyes drifted shut. He heard Owen breathing lightly at his side before he shifted.

"I want to buy the bar from Mr. Yorke. He used to

pick me up and bring me here after school let out since Mom always had to work late, so I've seen this place go from humble beginnings to... all of this." Owen motioned to the spacious room. "To be able to run it myself and keep this piece of my history alive would be amazing."

A woman's sing-song voice called his name, "Lukas? Lukas, we're leaving! Where'd you go?"

"Ah, that's Sienna. That's right, I'm carpooling with her and Archer." Lukas groaned as he sat up, his back hurting from resting in a weird position.

"I still have an hour or so. I'll meet you back at the apartment."

Deep down, Lukas knew he'd have to go back to his house eventually. He sighed, rubbing his temples.

"Actually, I need to... I can't keep loafing at your place forever."

"I understand, say no more, but I'm not leaving you alone at your place until you're comfortable. I'm gonna go back to the apartment and grab the critters and some clothes, and I'll meet you, okay?"

"But–"

"No. Babe, please. Just until I know you're not afraid to be alone in your own house. I can see you shaking right now."

Lukas leaned forward, resting his elbows on his knees.

"Alright, alright. I get it. We're a team. We do this together, right?"

"Exactly." Owen beamed, wrapping his arm around Lukas and pulling him close.

"Luuuuukas!?" Sienna's voice pierced the quiet room.

With a sigh, Lukas stood in front of his alpha, bending over to kiss his mate.

"I want to thank you for putting up with

everything that's been going on recently. I know it's been a mess, but you've stuck around through it all."

"Don't thank me, love. I know it's been hard, and there have been some scary moments, but I wouldn't trade all of this for the world," Owen replied, gazing up into Lukas' eyes with a loving smile. "Now get going. I think Sienna's gonna tear the building down looking for you."

Lukas chuckled at the thought of the tiny, four-foot-tall woman punching through brick and mortar, her little sidekick next to her, copying her every move. He would definitely pay to see that.

Lukas snuck in another quick kiss and headed for the breakroom door. He knew he had a dorky smile on his flushed face, and he knew he would be questioned when he rejoined his group, but did he care? No. No, he didn't.

"I am omega, hear me roar," Lukas whispered to himself.

"I still can't believe you left me at the bar, Sienna. I may never forgive you." Lukas crossed his arms and pouted, his face illuminated by the passing street lights as Archer weaved through traffic.

"Ya big baby, yer fine. I knew ya were so worried about bothering Owen, you wouldn't go over to the bar yerself. All ya needed was a friend to get ya over there, and everything turned out grrreat," Sienna giggled quietly, pleasantly warm from the drinks she had shared with her old friends.

The music coming from the radio suddenly got quieter as Archer's voice drifted from the front seat. "You said you're going back to your house tonight, right Lukas?"

"Yeah. Owen said he'd meet me there after he picks up the creatures and some clothes."

Sienna giggled.

"You know what creature I want? One of those, uh… farty cats."

He heard Archer snicker in the front seat before it hit him. He immediately flashed back to the time he tried to free a skunk from a trap in fourth grade. You bet your ass he regretted that decision. Colton never let him live that one down.

"Trust me, you don't want a farty cat, Sienna. Regret smells like rotten eggs," Lukas murmured.

"No, no, I think we should get her one, Lukas. I mean, her birthday *is* coming up in July." Archer looked up into the rearview mirror with a smile.

Lukas crossed his arms and leaned back against the seat. His eyes wandered to the window, tuning out Sienna's rambling. Familiar buildings started flitting by in the dark streets until the car slowly pulled to a stop.

Archer threw the car into park, relaxing in his seat for a few moments.

"Well, home sweet home. Thanks for coming out with us tonight, Lukas. I'm gonna get little miss crazy home before she starts wanting spiny pigs or actor rats.

Lukas froze mid-climb out of the car and looked back in at Archer.

"What?"

"Porcupines or possums," Archer whispered with a wide grin.

Sienna, suddenly gaining supersonic hearing, gasped loudly, "Actor rats. Oh my… the Shakespeares of the highway!"

"Run, Lukas! I'll hold her off!" Archer quickly rolled up the windows, pressing the lockdown button on his door. "I have only one final request. Bring donuts to my grave!"

Archer pulled away from the curb without listening for Lukas' reply, and peeled off down the road.

Lukas shook his head and smiled as he reached his front door and stepped inside his suddenly unfamiliar house. It hadn't been that long since he had been here, right?

Darkness filled almost every corner of his house save for the kitchen where everyone had gathered after the cleanup. Oops. He must have forgotten that light when he and Owen left a few days ago. His gaze lingered on the stairs, knowing he would have to make the trip to the second floor sooner or later.

Locking the door behind him, Lukas carefully made his way up. Glancing to his right, he saw brand new frames holding his photos. His family smiled back at him from behind the clean glass.

Reaching his bedroom, he steeled himself as he pushed open the door. Okay. Step one complete. He stood at the edge of his moonlit bedroom for the first time since the attack. He needed to do this. He had to know that Aaron really wasn't here anymore, that Owen had won.

Taking a deep breath, he walked across the spotless floor, reaching the window where he had first caught the scent of Aaron. He pulled it open, and a cool breeze drifted in, making the curtains dance around him. His nose crinkled, catching the faint scent of Aaron still left in the room.

Lukas' ears twitched as he heard the roar of an engine coming closer and closer. Resting his elbows on the windowsill, he carefully looked in the direction of the noise.

"And there he is," Lukas whispered to himself. He

quickly went downstairs to unlock the door, more than ready to get out of the bitter-scented room for a few minutes.

After unpacking the critters and lugging a couple of suitcases to the bedroom, Lukas trembled from a mix of crisp air and the reminders of the attack still wafting around the room. He walked over to the open window, hugging himself as he looked into the dark streets.

"It's still scary, isn't it?" Owen's voice drifted across the room.

Lukas' skin tingled.

"I can still smell him," Lukas whispered.

"You can stay at my apartment as long as you need to, babe. You know that."

"I need this closure. I need to know that he's actually gone and that you're...." Lukas ran his fingers over the bite mark on his neck, shuddering.

Lukas tensed when he felt Owen's arms wrap around his shoulders from behind. The alpha had a cozy blanket draped over his arms, and he covered them both in the fleecy fabric. Lukas felt Owen kiss the still-healing bite on his neck.

Leaning into the embrace, Lukas suddenly felt himself turn around and get pinned between the wall and a warm body, wrapped in his alpha's strong arms. His heart pounded, and he felt a gentle warmth spread through his body as he lost himself in the embrace.

"Whatever you need, I'll provide," Owen breathed softly before kissing Lukas.

Lukas moaned. Each kiss was slowly numbing his mind, any anxiety slowly melting away.

Owen let out a faint, heated growl, pulling his omega closer. He framed his arms on the wall around Lukas' head.

"You've got the reins, babe. What do you need me to do for you?" Owen gazed down at Lukas, licking his lips.

Lukas slowly pushed himself off the wall, pushing Owen backward toward his bed.

Owen got the idea and guided them carefully back onto the soft mattress, pulling Lukas on top of him.

"Help me wipe out his scent. I want no trace of him left in here," Lukas said in a firm voice, tightening his legs around Owen's hips.

A feral growl escaped Owen's lips as his hips bucked up, and he dragged Lukas down for a deep kiss.

"My scent will cover you and fill you. No other alpha will bother you again," Owen growled as he quickly worked Lukas' shirt off, tossing it across the room. Owen grabbed Lukas' hips and dragged him down, earning a stifled moan from the sudden friction.

"Pants. Off. Now," Lukas moaned quietly with each movement. Fire coursed through the omega's veins as he felt dirty, slick, and empty once more.

"Alpha, please. Please, I need you."

It didn't take long for Lukas to find himself under Owen, grasping his pillow for leverage.

He felt Owen shift above him as he was filled. He moaned into the pillow as the alpha moved. Lukas pushed back against Owen, compelling him to move faster. Owen grabbed Lukas' hips, pulling the omega back with each thrust.

Getting lost in pleasure, Lukas whimpered as he felt heat building up in his stomach. Owen's hand cradled his chest, holding him up from behind as his own arms trembled beneath him. He felt Owen's warm lips on the back of his shoulder and neck, teeth nipping the tender flesh.

Owen groaned as he suddenly pulled out and flipped Lukas over. Seeing his omega exposed like this was maddening. He pushed one of Lukas' legs up and pumped the omega's cock in time with his own thrusts.

"Can't smell him anymore. Only you. My mate, my beautiful omega," Owen growled, pushing Lukas' other leg up.

Lukas' hand roamed down to pick up the task that Owen had left behind.

"God, just look at you," Owen purred, looking down at Lukas.

Heat flooded Lukas' body as he gazed up at Owen. His alpha. His protector.

"Stake your claim, alpha," Lukas moaned, pumping his own cock faster as he leaned his head back into the pillows.

Owen leaned forward as Lukas came, biting the raw spot on the crook of his neck. He groaned as Lukas tightened around him, his cock swelling painfully.

Their moans and pants filled the quiet room, the cooling breeze from the windows flitting across their bodies. Owen looked down at Lukas, the moonlight hitting his omega at such an angle that his eyes glowed beautifully.

"Claim staked." Owen mumbled, licking the small trails of blood coming from the bite mark.

Lukas squirmed faintly at the alpha's tongue gliding across the sensitive wound. His legs locked behind Owen's hips, dragging him closer. Lukas whimpered when he felt the alpha go deeper.

Owen hissed quietly, "Careful, babe, don't hurt yourself."

"*I'm sorry, it just feels so good,*" Lukas mewled, nuzzling into Owen's chest before slowly grinding on the alpha again.

"You're so wound up." Owen groaned before bucking his hips lightly.

"Guess this means we're staying here tonight," Lukas whispered.

Lukas planted kisses on Owen's neck as he rolled his hips down, drawling out, "*Stay as long as you want. I don't mind one bit.*"

A low chuckle hit Lukas' ears as he felt himself being dragged up from the warmth of the sheets.

"Buckle up, love. It's gonna be a looooong night," Owen whispered.

CHAPTER 13

A quiet alarm on his phone roused him from his sleep. Not that he actually slept well, anyway. He had tossed and turned all night, despite the fact that his entire body felt like lead.

He didn't want to wake Owen this early if he could help it. He rolled onto his back and stared at the ceiling. It was still dark outside, and his body just wasn't having it. His eyes burned with exhaustion, and his arms trembled as he leaned up on his elbows.

The days had slipped through his fingers as he tried to get back into the groove of normal, everyday life. Now, it was the day of Hazel's party, and he was dreadfully unprepared.

Lukas closed his eyes and slowly exhaled. He didn't have time to laze about. He had so much to do before this party. The poor girl would be so disappointed if he didn't show up.

Hearing Owen's snores to his right, Lukas felt his focus drifting. Owen had been staying with him for the last week, much to his delight. They had spent the days enjoying the finer points of life: good food, comfy clothes, and a mess of fervid embraces. He felt more at ease when his alpha was nearby, but Owen had to go back to his apartment eventually.

"Just a few more minutes," Lukas groaned as he reset the alarm on his phone for fifteen minutes. The soft embrace of his quilt surrounded him as he sank back into the mattress.

LUKAS AWOKE LATER WITH THE LIGHT OF THE LATE morning sun warming his bedroom. He cracked open his eyes and groaned. Muffled music reached his ears, and he shielded his face with his arm. There was a warm weight pressing down on his body. Looking down, he saw Miss Mulberry basking on his stomach, acting as if she owned the place.

He tried to focus his vision as it finally dawned on him. Oh crap.

"The cake! Fu–! Already ten!?" Lukas shot up, accidentally launching Miss Mulberry across the bed.

A clatter in the kitchen startled the already panicking omega. Miss Mulberry darted at the sound, hastily retreating in an unknown direction. It was then that he noticed the sweet scent of baked goods drifting throughout the house. Standing warily, he wrapped the sun-warmed blanket around his shoulders and made his way downstairs, curious.

As he leaned against the doorframe, Lukas was stunned. His kitchen was in shambles. Owen was rocking out to quiet music on a small radio and stumbling around the unfamiliar kitchen. Countless pots and pans soaked in the sink, ingredients were scattered across the counters, and…

Lukas covered his mouth, trying to hold back a chuckle. He wanted to watch Owen in his unnatural habitat just a bit longer, but he accidentally caught the attention of Mimosa.

"I could have sworn Mimosa was a Golden Retriever, not a White Lab."

Owen flinched at the sudden voice, spinning around in a flash.

The poor dog was completely covered in flour. As she wagged her tail at the mention of her name, she flung some of the dust on Owen.

"Well, you see, she thought it was a good idea to get all up in my way when I was holding the tin of flour and then…" Owen motioned to his now white pant leg. "She insisted on returning the favor. It was a vicious cycle that only ended once we ran out of flour."

Crossing his arms, Lukas put a grim look on his face, sighing.

"So, would you say you two are all dressed up and have nowhere to dough?"

A gasp reached Lukas' ears.

"You. Did. Not," a low voice muttered. "Oh my, God, I've rubbed off on you." Owen's giddy voice trailed off as he leaned back against the counter, staring up at the ceiling with a smile.

Lukas' eyes trailed to three cake pans that rested on the counter near the window.

"Is that…?"

"I didn't want to wake you. Well, actually, I couldn't. You were one-hundred percent out of it, but your instructions were very detailed. At first, I wasn't sure if I was doing it right. Then it turned into something amazing." Owen threw a kitchen towel over his shoulder and cracked his knuckles. "I'm just waiting for them to cool so it can be put together and frosted–"

Owen froze when he felt Lukas drag him into a hug. The warm fleece blanket surrounded their bodies, making the already stuffy kitchen almost unbearable. Almost.

Carefully winding his arms around Lukas, Owen felt a smile tugging at his lips. This was how it was meant to be, just him, Lukas, and the critters. What more could he ask for?

"Like I said, we're a team now, love. You don't have to do it all yourself."

"Yep. You're stuck with me, you big goof. Your fate has been sealed." Lukas grinned. "Now come on. We only have an hour to finish this up and get to Sienna's."

THE SQUEAL OF BRAKES AND AN ENGINE SHUTTING down roused Lukas from his unintended nap. Looking outside the car window, he saw the small house Sienna and Hazel called home. It was a quaint house just north of West Roxbury, framed by a perfectly manicured yard.

Lukas felt Owen's hand on his leg, squeezing it lightly before he got out of the car.

"Come on, sleepyhead. We have delight to deliver."

Following suit, Lukas grabbed the wrapped gifts from behind his seat, and Owen carried the cake.

Stepping up to the side door that led into the kitchen, Lukas heard the delighted squeals of children coming from the backyard. He saw Sienna at her stove, jamming out to a muffled song. She definitely wouldn't hear them knocking.

Nudging open the door, he carefully maneuvered himself through, then held it for Owen. They slid past the few parents who were still dawdling in the kitchen, hoping to grab a bit of food before they left.

A warm summer breeze drifted through the

nearby open window. Streamers hung from every corner of the house, mimicking the gentle movement of the tide as the gust danced through the rooms. Ocean-related trinkets and baubles littered every room, and a hidden phone played tropical music.

The serene moment was shattered when the back door flew open, hitting the wall behind it. Three young girls scampered through the hallway and kitchen, bumping into people, before darting back outside, laughing the entire way. About that time, the remaining parents decided it was an excellent time to head out, and they quickly thanked Sienna for her hospitality and fled to their cars.

Poor Sienna looked so frazzled. She immediately threw down her spatula and gathered Lukas into a hug.

"About time you two showed up. I thought they were going to eat me alive!"

"Sienna, they're little girls, not crazed carnivorous beasts," Owen snickered.

"Well, you didn't see the way they were eyeing these burgers and hotdogs." Sienna motioned to her stove, her hand on her hip. "I swear they were sizing me up to see if they could get me out of the way."

"I mean, they do smell fantastic. Might have to smack me with a spatula too," Lukas said.

"Why, I would never…!"

Sienna cut herself off mid-sentence when she saw Owen inching closer to the stove. Quick as a flash, she smacked Owen, and shooed him away.

Owen cradled his injured hand with a mock pout.

"I thought you said you wouldn't smack!"

"Never said I wouldn't smack you. As punishment for your sassiness, you are hereby designated as the impromptu party game director. Hop to it!" Sienna pointed outside.

"But–" Owen protested.

"Go! Anyone who dares steal from my kitchen is banished until further notice."

Owen skulked outside, and Lukas felt a shiver run down his spine when Sienna turned to him.

"And you. I need your baking expertise. Help me finish up these cupcakes, please."

"Cupcakes *and* cake? Are you insane?"

"Nah, I'm feeling lucky," Sienna tossed a wooden spoon to him and motioned to the pantry.

Losing track of time was easy as he baked to his heart's content. He made enough cupcakes to feed a small army, which was quite fortunate, considering there was a small army of mermaids and sea creatures just mere feet away.

Lukas watched as twelve young girls dressed in bright colors and adorned with plastic jewelry circled Owen. Or, more specifically, circled the circle of chairs Owen was standing in.

He balanced a small boom box on his shoulder as he twisted and shifted along to the tunes, waiting for the best, or worst, time to stop the song and send the young girls scrambling for a chair.

Lukas thought to himself as he idly watched the spectacle. It reminded him of a nature documentary he had watched a few months back.

"They circle and circle, closing in ever-so-slightly, waiting to strike," Lukas said absent-mindedly while waiting on some cupcakes to come out of the oven.

"What are you talking about?" Sienna questioned, coming over to watch the spectacle. Giggling, she pried open the window further and stuck her head out.

"Little baby sharks!" She leaned out the window and yelled, "Better watch out, Owen, their teeth are sharp!"

"What!?" Owen yelled back, spinning around to pinpoint the voice over the music in his ear.

This action proved to be his downfall, as the boombox almost slipped from his shoulders. His fingers brushed the buttons, effectively silencing the music. All at once, twelve little girls scrambled to get to the last seashell chairs, and one girl flew into a chair and sent it toppling back into Owen.

"Oh, sea biscuits, I'm hit!" Owen yelled. He theatrically dropped to the ground before being covered by a giggling dogpile of children.

"Think we should rescue him?" Sienna asked.

"I don't think there's any hope of rescue. He knew the dangers of this party before he set foot into your yard. His fate is in their hands now."

"I think not, Lukas. They may be numerous, and they may be ravenous, but I am the true master of the party, and they respond to my command."

"How? They've already taken down an alpha, and that isn't even their final form. How will you get them to listen to you?" Lukas asked.

"Simple, my minion. Simple."

Sienna rubbed her hands together.

"Alright, girls, grub's on!" Sienna yelled out the window.

Lukas watched as the girls scrambled off the wounded alpha, eager to devour their food before the presents were opened. As the dust settled, he heard Owen groan. Sienna hadn't been lying when she said these little girls were ferocious.

Lukas smiled as he saw Hazel stand next to Owen, looking down at him. She extended her small hand down to the alpha.

"Oh, little princess, you've come to my rescue." Lukas heard Owen say as he stretched out on the grass before carefully sitting up.

"I can't leave you out here. You have to help us eat all this food," Hazel grinned, pulling on his shirt sleeve until he stood up. "Besides, I know Lukas would be sad if you stayed out here all day."

"Can't argue with you there, kiddo. I'd be sad if I had to stay outside all day away from him, too," Owen snickered. He let the little girl lead him toward the house.

"Come on, Mama's gonna start without us!" Hazel tugged on Owen's hand, dragging him toward the side door.

"Oh, goodness, we can't have that!"

Lukas smiled as Owen picked up his pace, ushering the girl into the house ahead of him.

"The princess has arrived!" Owen announced mimicking fanfare with a nearby empty paper towel roll. "Let the festivities begin!"

LUKAS SIGHED, SLIPPING HIS APRON OVER HIS HEAD AND folding it. Wait. Not his apron, thankfully. Neon pink really wasn't his color; it didn't do anything for his complexion. He had borrowed Sienna's apron since he hadn't expected to do any baking outside of his house.

The girls were finally fed and happy, having eaten as fast as they could so they could open gifts as soon as possible. Now they just had to finish dessert. Lukas gladly took this moment of peace to lean back against the counter, careful not to disturb the leftover food.

"You should eat, babe. You didn't have anything this morning before we left. I promise you, Sienna is not a bad cook," Owen whispered, smirking when Sienna waved her spatula at him.

Owen leaned back against the counter next to Lukas before biting into his burger.

"I know she's good now, but I was her guinea pig for a while when she first started cooking, and that's something you never forget," Lukas grimaced.

"Maybe you can get a bit of rest in before they start opening gifts?"

"I can't leave you and Sienna alone with an entire army sitting in this kitchen, especially not when they're about to hit a sugar high," Lukas said.

Lukas jumped when Sienna suddenly appeared next to him.

"Go rest, you doof. I command thee." She pointed to the hallway. "Guest room is calling your name, so go make yourself comfy. I'll come get you when they start opening gifts."

"But–"

Lukas' words caught in his throat when Sienna's motherly gaze turned ice-cold.

"Yes, ma'am," Lukas squeaked. His voice was suddenly small as he retreated to the guest room, leaving Owen with a quick kiss. He heard Sienna put Owen in charge of snack distribution as he entered the guest room.

Exhaling slowly, Lukas closed the door behind him, leaning against it for a moment before stepping further into the homey bedroom.

"Still looks the same."

He had spent a lot of time in this room when he first came to Boston. Memories started flowing back as he sat on the bed. He fell back, leaving his legs dangling over the edge. His eyes drifted shut. He knew the noise outside would never allow him to go into a deep sleep, but he felt his muscles slowly relax, his only company being his thoughts.

It really had been five years. He had practically

watched Hazel grow up. He had his own place, a job he loved, and now his dork of an alpha.

Time stretched on, and the most bizarre thoughts flitted through his mind as sleep crept closer. He knew he was close to falling asleep whenever he lost his train of thought mid-thought. It was as simple as going, going, gon–

Lukas' eyes shot open as he felt a surge of nausea wash over him. Not thinking, he rushed out of the room to the bathroom across the hall. He heard a clamor in the kitchen as he accidentally slammed the door.

He didn't remember getting sick. The next thing he knew, Sienna was rubbing his back and asking Owen to keep an eye on the girls.

"You never get sick, Lukas. Did you eat anything funny?" Sienna asked.

"I actually haven't eaten anything in a couple of days. I've been too tired to really be hungry," Lukas said.

Sienna froze, eyeing the bite on Lukas' neck.

"Have you checked your mark?"

Lukas tensed up and leaned back against the tub as he felt the last wave of nausea pass. "I haven't. You don't think…?"

"May I check?" Sienna whispered.

Lukas carefully turned around, exposing his back to his friend, shuddering at the sudden chill on his skin.

"Oh, my God, I'm gonna be an auntie," Sienna said warmly. She lightly traced her finger around the mark on the back of Lukas' shoulder blade.

"How's it look?" Lukas asked.

"It's a brilliant shade of red. You're a few weeks along, at least. Maybe a month." Sienna smiled, hugging Lukas.

The world seemed to get brighter as it finally hit him. Lukas didn't know whether his pounding heart meant joy or fear. Maybe both.

"Oh, Owen… When should we tell him? Shit, how is he going to react?"

"He probably already knows, but tell him as soon as you get out of this bathroom, you doofball! He's gonna be ecstatic!" Sienna pulled Lukas to his feet.

Wobbling, Lukas grasped the sink to balance his weight. He didn't feel like crushing Sienna in her own bathroom. That would require too much paperwork.

"Go rest for a while longer. I'll sneak you some Sprite and crackers." Sienna pushed him back toward the guest room.

"About that…" Lukas snickered as he saw Owen come around the corner.

"Who's watching the kids?" Sienna asked warily, narrowing her eyes.

"Andre and Dahlia showed up, don't worry. They started opening gifts already," Owen said. "Are you okay, love?"

"I'm okay. Just need a bit of rest." Lukas wrapped his arms around Owen's waist, resting his head against the other man's chest.

The sound of rustling paper came from the kitchen, with excited voices following.

"She must have found the Merida doll," Sienna giggled.

"Mama, look what Mammy and Papaw got me." Hazel ran around the corner, skidding to a stop to avoid running into Owen. She held up the doll in the box to show Lukas and Owen. "Look!"

"Very beautiful, sweetie. Mammy knew you'd like that." Sienna pulled Hazel into a hug.

Hazel seemed to notice that Lukas wasn't quite himself.

"Are you okay? Mama said to stay out of the bathroom when she ran off. Did you get sick?"

Lukas' eyes burned with fatigue, but he realized his body was humming with positive energy.

"I'm okay. Don't worry about me right now. You should get back to your friends. They're waiting for you."

Hazel beamed as she sprinted back to the kitchen, prepared to open more gifts. Owen waited until he heard the sound of wrapping paper being torn up before he sighed.

"So, what's going on? You both are acting stranger than normal," Owen's gaze drifted between the omegas.

Sienna and Lukas exchanged looks before Lukas smiled and took Owen's hands in his.

"I'm pregnant."

Owen was silent for a moment before a wide smile flashed across his face.

"So, it's true! I thought my eyes were deceiving me. I mean, I caught a glimpse of your mark a few days ago. I thought it looked a bit swollen, but–!"

He squeezed Lukas against him in a tight hug before whispering apologies and loosening his grip.

"You won't break him, Owen. Trust me. Squeeze to your heart's content," Sienna smiled.

Another squeal came from the kitchen.

"And there's the Jack Skellington action figure set." Sienna looked at her imaginary wristwatch. "Three, two, one."

"I got the skeleton, Mama." The girl looked positively stoked as she ran around the corner to show off her new toy before she whispered sadly, "But my friends don't know what movie he's from."

"They don't know what they're missing out on, sweetpea." Sienna looked back at Owen and Lukas.

Hazel's gaze bounced between the three. "So why are you hanging out here? Are you sure you're okay?"

"Better than okay, short-stuff." Owen crouched down to her level. "We're gonna have a short-stuff of our own."

"You and Lukas are gonna be daddies? When?" Hazel held Sienna's hand as she bounced with excitement.

"Sometime around January or February, we think," Lukas whispered.

Hazel grinned, running up to hug Lukas. "You're gonna do good. You'll be good daddies, just like mine."

A small choked noise came from Sienna as she turned away for a moment. Lukas worked quickly to keep Hazel's attention on him and Owen.

The girl reached up to her neck and opened her locket to reveal a small family portrait Lukas had seen countless times, and she showed it to Owen.

"That's my daddy. I guess he spoke a bit weird because people would always talk about his voice. I think mama said he was from brit… British?"

Sienna's voice was quiet. "Great Britain. His name was Kieran Adgate."

A pale man with dark hair held Sienna close in the picture. A beautiful toddler smiled broadly, cradled by both parents in the center.

"He was a good man. You must miss him a lot, Hazel," Lukas whispered.

"Yeah. I wish he could be here, so mama didn't have to worry so much." Hazel looked down at the locket, smiling. "Mama? Can we go show Daddy my new dolls later?"

Sienna had composed herself, quickly putting on a smile.

"Of course, sweetie. Once everything winds down around here, we'll head out there. Now head on back to the table. I'm sure your friends miss you."

"They all went outside. We already opened everything, so Mammy and Papaw are gonna play with us! Thank you for the food, Mama." Hazel hugged her mom before turning to Lukas and Owen.

"And it better be a girl! We have too many boys at my school right now!"

Lukas laughed. "Yes, ma'am. We'll do our best."

The house was suddenly quiet as Hazel ran out the side door, eager to play with her friends. Sienna pulled both men into a hug.

"Thank you so much for all your help today. Both of you. I think I'm gonna get everything cleaned up, and then I'll take Hazel over to the cemetery."

"We'll hel–" Lukas started.

"Don't you dare offer to stay and help clean up. You've done enough. Go home and get some rest, you doof."

"I see how it's gonna be." Lukas crossed his arms, smiling.

Sienna giggled, jabbing Lukas' arm.

"Go on. You two have a lot to discuss and plan for."

Owen peppered butterfly kisses all over the side of Lukas' face. "And we have to get ready for the Heated Hullabaloo too. It's in five days."

"Oh, you're right!" Lukas gasped, looking at the clock. "It's already four, and we need to restock. More flour, eggs, sugar…"

"And so it shall be." Owen grinned.

Lukas started dragging Owen to the side door. Pulling it open, he turned and pointed at Sienna,

"You better be there. Don't you try to weasel out of this one. I know where you live."

Sienna gasped dramatically.

"But… how?" she asked, casually glancing around before smirking. "Get out of here, punk. Go do your thing." She pushed them lightly toward the door, picking up wrapping paper on the way, and tossing it in a trash bag.

"And don't worry, I'll be there!" she yelled as they were almost to the car.

Owen whistled as they settled down in his car. Gripping the steering wheel, he asked, "Where to, babe?"

"There's this great supermarket over near Codman Square." Lukas smiled, making a list in his head as Owen fired up the engine.

"What's so great about it, exactly?" Owen asked.

"We can bother my friend Eliseo if he's working." Lukas gave a thumbs up. "Now go, go, go!"

"Yes, dear." Owen chuckled, and pulled away from the curb.

CHAPTER 14

"That's good. Just a bit harder. Keep at it." Lukas felt the sweat rolling down his neck. It was way too hot in here.

He heard Owen's breath hitch as he moved a bit faster.

"Perfect. Just like that. Just a little more. Careful not to get it all over you. It's a bit sticky," Lukas purred.

"Uh, babe?" Owen shakily asked.

"What's wrong? Don't stop for too long." Lukas stared at his mate with half-lidded eyes.

"You're doing this on purpose." Owen's eyes narrowed. His arm was frozen mid-stir, batter dripping from his wooden spoon. A predatory smirk settled on his lips. "What? Are we stars in a cheesy porn movie now?"

Lukas gasped, covering his mouth. "I can assure you; I have no idea what you're talking about."

"Yeah, I know exactly what you're doing, just like you know we have guests coming over soon. I'm hurt. Absolutely devastated. I love hanging out with people, but just for today, damn our social gatherings."

"And why is that?"

Owen put down the bowl of batter he was mixing and slowly crowded Lukas up against the kitchen island, placing his arms on both sides of the omega.

"Because all that talk, that scent. I would love nothing more than to shove all this food to the side, and let it clatter to the floor. I just wanna bend you over this island and–"

The obnoxiously loud doorbell, followed by Mimosa's barking, startled both men.

Lukas gripped Owen's shirt hard, tucking his head under the alpha's chin. Owen growled low in his throat before releasing Lukas and calming himself, closing his eyes and taking a deep breath.

"It's getting everywhere," Lukas whispered.

Owen cracked open his eyes, glancing warily.

"Your batter. Fruit of your loi–" Lukas cleared his throat. "–labor," he smiled innocently.

Before Owen could reply, the doorbell rang again, and again, before finally, it became a continuous string of noise.

"Eliseo, I'll be there in a minute, for Pete's sake!" Lukas yelled over the chimes.

A muffled voice came from the other side of the door, "You know–"

Lukas pulled open the door, allowing the full force of Eliseo's voice to pierce the house.

"– how I feel about Pete, Lukas!" Eliseo grinned as he fell forward through the doorway dramatically, languidly draping his arms over Lukas' shoulders to balance himself.

His grin was short-lived. A yelp escaped his lips as a young Asian man cuffed him lightly over the head.

"You're too loud, Eliseo. I swear, one day, that mouth of yours is going to get you into trouble."

"Why're you like that, Sawyer? I'll have you know,

my mouth has made a lot of people happy." Eliseo stuck out his tongue at the passing man, arms crossed.

Sawyer cringed, turning to face Eliseo with a look of shock.

"Get your mind out of the gutter," Eliseo laughed. "Anyway, we have brought offerings." He turned to Lukas.

"Offerings? What for?" Lukas asked, peeking in the bags and boxes Sawyer was hauling in.

Owen rushed off to help as Eliseo gaped.

"You're joking, right? Nobody told you?"

"Oh, you're right. It completely slipped my mind. I forgot today was the annual sacrifice to the ancestors of Purrgak-ron, The Seventh! Why, I should be publicly whipped and shamed for that slight!"

"Okay, I don't know what sort of stuff you and Owen are into, but it's nothing like that." Sawyer gave a wary side-look, then stepped back into the house. "By the way, look who we found creeping around outside." Sawyer motioned with his head back toward the door.

"Greetings to the happy couple." Archer stepped halfway through the doorway, waving. "I have brought company, and we both brought food. You may thank us now." Archer bowed quickly.

Turning back, Archer dragged Mr. Yorke into the house, barely giving the man time to exchange pleasantries with Lukas and Eliseo. Mimosa followed the two men closely, sticking close to Mr. Yorke.

"Now, have we got a treat for you two." Archer clapped his hands together. "But first, introducing the lovely Sienna, and her peppy teenybopper, Hazel!"

Hazel bounded into the house, zooming past

Archer and Eliseo to hug Lukas. A soft wheeze drifted from his mouth as something hard dug into his side. He looked down and saw the face of the Merida doll squished between Hazel and him.

"Hazel, manners, sweetie! Don't go rushing around when there are so many people walking!" Sienna called out, dropping some bags off in the living room.

"Don't forget us! Dahlia Debonair and Andre Affable!" a woman's voice cackled over the ruckus of the living room. Hazel released her grip on Lukas and ran to greet her grandparents.

Archer gasped, placing both hands on his face. "She outdid me in the name game. I am not worthy."

The man quickly scampered over to Dahlia, kowtowing before her.

"Teach me your ways, Mistress of the Gift of Gab."

The once silent house was filled with voices and chatter. In the fuss, Owen had managed to squeeze through everyone to stand next to Lukas.

"I'm gonna cowbell them," Lukas whispered just loud enough so Owen could hear.

"What? Now is not the time to be dirty."

"No, I'm literally gonna." Lukas snuck off to the kitchen and returned with an item cradled delicately in his hands so it wouldn't make noise prematurely.

"No way." Owen grinned widely. "Do it. Do it now."

Lukas swung the cowbell with all his might and cringed at the deafening noise that came from it. The chatter in the living room died down instantly, and everyone stared in shock at the couple.

Lukas' giggles died down as he said, "I know we invited everyone over to help prepare for the Heated Hullabaloo, and I'm so glad you all are here, but what is all of this?" His eyes flitted across the pile of gifts in the corner of the living room and the boxes of decorations in the entryway.

Sawyer carefully carried a vase of flowers in his arms, gingerly placing it on the coffee table in the living room.

"Well, take a look at this. Notice the lisianthus, it's a symbol of an everlasting bond. Next, the stock flowers, which symbolize a happy life. And need I point out the filler flowers?

"Baby's breath?" Lukas asked.

"Well, we heard a certain someone was expecting. It would be a sin to not include such simple, meaningful flowers," Sawyer casually mentioned. He stooped down to pet Miss Mulberry, who was rubbing against his leg.

Owen chuckled, wrapping his arm around Lukas' waist. He cast a glance at Sienna, who was still standing in the entryway. "My, word travels fast."

Sienna glared at Owen, "Why must you assume it was me? You wound me, for the true culprit is—"

"Me!"

Archer choked, almost dropping his water bottle on the floor. He gasped, "Surely not!"

Hazel had her arm raised high as she skittered about the living room, "I told Eliseo! Mama and I met him at the store a few days ago. He made a new dress for my doll."

"So, Eliseo is the true culprit." Lukas sighed.

Eliseo looked sheepish, shrugging with a grin. "Um, surprise?"

Rubbing his hands together, Mr. Yorke stepped forward.

"We have discovered that there is a miscreant in our midst, but there is a more urgent situation at hand."

With a charming smile, he motioned to the bare living room.

"I see a spacious room that is in dire need of some fitting decorations for this upcoming event. At this moment, I feel that young Hazel, Sawyer, Eliseo, and Andre would be most proficient at creating a homely venue for our ceremony."

"And what about the rest of us, Master?" Archer taunted, arching his eyebrow.

Mr. Yorke thought for a moment. "Well, I was going to say the rest of us will handle the cooking for now, but your lip has just landed you on decorating duty."

The bartender clapped his hand on Archer's back, laughing, before he led Lukas, Owen, Dahlia, and Sienna to the kitchen.

"Godspeed, my friend."

Archer shouted after the group, "Lukas? Sienna? Are you two just gonna leave me out here? No, wait, wait..."

Archer cleared his throat. "Surely, you jest?" he asked, butchering Mr. Yorke's accent. The man threw his patented puppy eyes at his employees, as if he was hoping they weren't numb to his antics after their years in his service.

Sienna stopped for a moment, turning slightly to face Archer. If the man had a tail, it would have been wagging like mad.

"Oh, Sienna, you do have a heart." Archer grinned widely, making eye contact with Mr. Yorke.

A flash of fire appeared in Sienna's dark eyes, silencing Archer. The woman cracked a smile, calling out, "Hazel, dear, please keep an eye on Archer. He'll be absolutely lost without us, and he may need some help."

Hazel giggled, grabbing Archer's arm as the man stood in shock. "Come on, we got stuff to do!"

I MUST HAVE BEEN HIGH OR SOMETHING. HE MUST HAVE been. How could he have been naïve enough to believe he could cook everything for the diner-bar combo booth himself?

He felt sweat run down the nape of his neck before he reached over and pulled open the small window in front of him, then he continued to cube the meat. He felt people rushing to and fro behind him, each working hard to complete their tasks.

Owen was to his right, trying to keep up with the piles of dishes and utensils heading his way. At the same time, Sienna and Dahlia focused on the stove, each working on a separate dish. Mr. Yorke was currently out, dropping off completed dishes at his bar to hold until the fair.

"Okay, so now we need to get all this caramel popcorn bagged!" Lukas called out to whoever was available. After dicing up the last of the meat, he quickly grabbed a new cutting board from the drain rack and began chopping up vegetables.

"On it," Sienna confirmed. "Mom, could you keep stirring this glaze, please?"

"Sure thing, kiddo." The old woman wielded dual wooden spoons like a champ, singing an old folk song as she tapped her foot in time.

"And then we need to get the meat for the skewers marinatin'. Ain't nothin' worse than bland, tough meat!" Lukas drawled, focusing on slicing the vegetables for the skewers.

"Sure thing, babe." Owen quickly took the meat and dropped it into a large bowl and filled it with sauces and spices.

"Finally, we need to glaze these cakes. Just imagine a beautiful, fragrant, fruit glaze dripping down the sides of the soft cake, topped with even more fresh fruit!"

Lukas' eyes had stars in them as he thought about the masterpiece. He felt like the head chef in a fancy Parisian kitchen, barking out where he needed people to be, what they needed to work on, and so forth.

"This berry filling for them pies is gonna be great, sugar," Dahlia called out from her spot at the stove where she was lightly stirring a berry mixture. "See? You treat your plants right, and they treat you right."

Grinning, Lukas dumped the chopped vegetables into a bowl for later. "I had hoped. Some good stuff happened in that garden."

Owen grinned widely as Lukas began to speak again.

Lukas looked at Owen before adding, "Lots of fertilizer, care, and such went into it. And that was where Owen and I had our first real heart-to-heart," Lukas smirked, hugging Owen from behind.

"And thus, it was blessed!" Owen announced loudly with a smile, holding the hands that were resting on his stomach.

"Aaaamen!" Dahlia whooped.

"Does this mean you're done cooking!? Archer is abusing me out here!" Eliseo's voice echoed from the living room.

"Not my fault you have delicate feelings!" Archer's voice followed.

"Lukas, you know I'm a very delicate individual! Send help!" Eliseo poked his head around the corner into the kitchen with Hazel right behind him. Mimosa bounded into the fray and sat next to Owen.

"Come on, Lukas, you have gifts to open!" Hazel

grinned eagerly.

"It'll be just a few minutes, Hazel," Lukas said.

A pout crossed Hazel's usually happy face before she said, "I'll just bring them here." She ran off before anyone could stop her and returned carrying a scraggly box.

"I wrapped this one myself. The ribbon didn't want to work with me, though," she said sullenly.

She hastened back to the living room, returning with three small bags.

"From Eliseo. But you should open mine first!"

The group exiled to the living room slowly filled the kitchen doorway, eager to see what Lukas got. Miss Mulberry hopped up onto a free chair near Lukas, ready to snatch any ribbons or paper he neglected to put away.

"Okay, okay. What do we have here?" Lukas took Hazel's gift and sat down at the one clear spot at the table. He delicately untied the beautiful ribbon wrapped around the box, putting it to the side. He tore the wrapping paper away and opened the box. He froze for a moment, staring at the contents.

"What's wrong? Do you not like it?" Hazel asked quietly, looking up at him.

Lukas lifted a stuffed elephant out of the box. He had seen it many times before. It was pale green, not at all fitting for an elephant, but still cute all the same. It was a little tattered with time, but the plush material was soft against his hands.

"Hazel, this is… are you sure?"

The girl nodded firmly. "Yeah, my daddy got it for me, but I wanted to give her to you. She'll make your baby happy. I know it!"

"Oh, Hazel, you and your heart." Lukas felt his eyes burn as he gathered the girl into a hug. "The baby'll love it."

"Well, this is good. Now you have the perfect test subject for my gift."

"What? Hold your horses, Dr. Frankenstein. I'm not going to be performing any crazy experiments on little Snerfie here." Lukas gripped the stuffed elephant, watching as Hazel made evil eyes at Eliseo.

"Oh, that did sound really ominous. I meant to say you have a practice model for my gift."

Lukas reached into the bags that Eliseo had brought and felt something soft. He carefully pulled out folded baby clothes, each piece picked out with care. Leave it to Eliseo to make sure the baby was fashionable.

"I didn't have enough time to make everything by hand as I would have liked, but if you turn your attention to the other bag..."

Lukas peeked into the other bag and spied something vibrant. He pulled the fabric out of the bag, careful to keep a hold on the gifts sitting on his lap.

It was a beautiful baby blanket with an elaborate menagerie of colorful animals covering the cloth. A soft ruffle lined the edges, and not a stitch was out of place.

"How in the world did you make this in two days?" Lukas asked.

"Let it be known that it took many bribes and many favors, but I stood victorious above the bolts of fabric by the end of it." Eliseo gave a thumbs up, looking very proud of himself.

Sawyer cleared his throat. "In other words, Rufio hooked him up."

"Hey, we all have a weakness. Mine just happens to be the sweet, sweet essence of the wakey-wakey bean," Eliseo said.

Hazel spoke up, interrupting the banter.

"Open the rest of your gifts, Lukas." The little girl smiled.

"I think you're more excited about this baby shower than you were about your birthday party." Owen laughed. "Come on then, babe. You've got some unwrapping to do. Especially that gift over there."

Owen pointed to the corner of the living room where a gift that was as big as the couch sat.

"When did that get there?" Lukas gasped.

"Never underestimate the abilities of a cook scorned. I channeled all my rage into carrying that gift in here while you lot were in the fray." Archer crossed his arms.

Sienna snickered as she closed up the last bag of popcorn.

"You wouldn't dare, Sienna." Archer glared.

"You don't know her as well as you think you do, son!" Dahlia cackled from the doorway.

"Dad, thank you so much for helping Archer carry that in," Sienna's tone was playful.

"Ain't no thing, dearie. I'm just happy to see that old thing go to a good place." Andre leaned back, relaxing into his spot on the couch.

Dahlia shuffled into the living room, taking a spot on the couch next to her husband.

"Save ours for last, darling. Archer looks like he's about to burst from anticipation, and I would so love to see what an antici-plosion looks like."

Archer visibly deflated. "Why is everyone picking on me today? I just want to know what was so heavy."

Lukas chuckled, moving to sit down in an armchair in the living room. Hazel quickly began piling gifts on his lap, restricting his movement.

"Don't worry. We'll find out soon enough, Boss."

· · ·

THE DIMMING SUNLIGHT CLUED LUKAS INTO HOW much time had passed before he even looked at the clock on his mantle. People would be out in full force on the roads fighting to get home by now.

He sighed. He was completely overwhelmed by everything that had happened in the last few weeks. Parties, fairs, meeting his fated mate, a new pregnancy. It was a lot to handle. Boxes full of clothing, books, and toys sat at Lukas' feet as he sank into his armchair.

Lukas' eyes closed as he listened to the catchy tunes coming from the TV speakers. Andre and Dahlia had already gone home for the evening, but the most varied, energetic trio who were still there were currently playing Just Dance. Owen and Sawyer worked quickly to carry everything upstairs to get it out of the way of the gamers, dodging the frenzied dancing of Hazel, Eliseo, and Archer.

"All the flailing in the world won't make your score go any higher, old man!" Eliseo jeered over the song.

"With age comes wisdom, my young friend," Archer said calmly.

"And wisdom is knowing that age is often detrimental to grace!" Eliseo retorted.

Lukas snickered as he listened to his friends bicker. They were so busy fighting, they didn't realize Hazel's score was rising steadily. He silently cheered the girl on as the game came to an end, undoubtedly naming the girl as the true master of 'Rasputin'.

A loud scrape on the hardwood floor startled everyone in the room. Owen and Sawyer were trying hard to move a sturdy crib from the corner of the living room without much success.

Sawyer grimaced. "Sorry, my noodly arms weren't prepared for this."

"Let me help. I need to do something to heal my injured pride." Archer stepped in to help.

"Still can't believe Andre made this himself. It's a beautiful piece." Sawyer's voice trailed off as he marveled at the craftsmanship.

Sienna smiled warmly, her face reliving every memory with that crib.

"Yeah, he made this for Hazel before she was born. The moment he found out Lukas was expecting, he got it out of storage and spent hours polishing it. You should have seen his face light up!"

Owen started backing up the steps, keeping a firm grip on the crib as Sienna followed behind, telling more stories about what her dad had made throughout the years.

"It is one-hundred percent appreciated, for sure. Everything is. And Eliseo making that blanket in two days? I can see why everyone speaks so highly of his skills."

"I know. I'm pretty awesome, right?" Eliseo grinned.

"What's your middle name, Eliseo?" Sawyer asked quietly.

"Esteban. Why?"

"So it's not humble. Glad we confirmed that." Sawyer nodded.

Eliseo stuck out his tongue, flipping a quick bird at Sawyer before returning to the living room for another quick dance-off with Hazel. Sawyer sighed and idly looked over the pictures hanging in the stairwell. His gaze landed on the old family photo that he had seen so many times.

The face of the teenager in the photo caught his attention. Lukas' older brother, Colton. Did he know? Lukas hadn't talked about his family in a long time, not since the first few months he was here in Boston.

Lukas made his way out of the living room, carrying Miss Mulberry, as the pair of dancers started up another song. Sawyer steeled himself, carefully piecing together what he thought his friend needed to hear.

"So, does Colton know? Have you told him yet?" Sawyer asked.

Lukas sighed, stroking his free hand through Miss Mulberry's fur. "No, he doesn't. I haven't spoken to him since I moved up here. I miss him, but it's just been so different since our parents died."

Sawyer gazed down at his friend. "You two used to be so close from what you've told me, so what are you afraid of?"

Silence drifted between the two before Lukas took a deep breath.

"You know I lived with him after they died, but he wasn't the same Colton I knew growing up. He had become so distant. It hit him hard after Ma and Pa died. He had to take on a lot all at once. He had to take care of me, our finances, and the funerals on top of taking care of himself. I think he's afraid to open up now. Doesn't want to go through that hurt again."

"See, that's what you think Colton is afraid of, but I asked what *you're* so worried about, Lukas."

Lukas was silent for a time.

"I'm afraid he won't give a damn. That I'll reach out and he won't give me the time of day. It'll be like losing Ma and Pa again. Gone just like that." He snapped his fingers.

"So, it's better to stay in limbo, forever, worrying about it than it is to know for sure?" Sawyer asked.

Hearing no response from his friend, Sawyer sighed.

"Lukas. Hear what I say. You and Colton, you've both already lost so much. Do you really want to lose each other over what could be a misunderstanding? What if he's sitting in a coffee shop right now thinking about how much he misses his little brother?"

"But–"

"Please, Lukas. You have a few days to think it over. And don't forget. You're not alone. You have a whole tsupport team behind you," Sawyer said.

Lukas sighed. Colton had always been a fun, strong, sometimes evil, older brother, but he had been Lukas' best friend growing up. He was scared, of course, but if he could have that same older brother back in his life again…

"Alright. I'll do it."

Sawyer perked up. "Really?"

"I mean, it'll be a mutual decision, but yeah." Lukas ran his fingers through Miss Mulberry's fur. "I miss him so much."

"No, no, no, don't cry, Lukas," Sawyer whispered. "Everything will go great. Just leave it to us. We'll get this done."

"Thanks, Sawyer." Lukas sniffed. "You spoil me, you know. All of you guys."

"You deserve it, Lukas." Sawyer smiled, giving his friend a hug. Miss Mulberry meowed softly as she was cradled by both warm bodies.

The peaceful calm in the house was shattered as Eliseo lost the last round of Just Dance. Hazel's delighted giggles echoed through the rooms as Sienna, Owen, and Archer started making their way downstairs.

"Sounds like Eliseo got his ass kicked," Archer said.

"Well, you did too, hotshot," Sienna snickered.

"You wound me. I wasn't in top form after carrying that crib in," Archer said.

"Aw, did you pull a muscle, old man?" Eliseo came around the corner into the entryway.

"You know what? I did. Help me to my car, young man," Archer teased.

The front door creaked open as Mr. Yorke arrived from his last trip to the bar just in time to see Archer using Eliseo's unwilling shoulders as a support beam.

"Sheldon, use the power of your accent to make Eliseo stand still! I'm an injured, old man. This is unfair."

Mr. Yorke chuckled, clearing his throat.

"If you're ready to go home, I will escort you, my friend. I am your driver for the day, after all." Mr. Yorke stepped through the door, holding it open for his 'crippled' friend. "No ifs, ands, or buts."

Archer planted his feet firmly on the ground, crossing his arms.

"Provided I leave with you now, you must use your accent on this bully, and promise to let me drink something when we get back to your bar. And I mean alcohol, not soda," Archer stated. "How's that for an if, and, or but?"

The room was silent as everyone stared at Archer in shock.

Archer himself was shocked by the silence, and he turned back to stare at everyone.

"What? You don't think old Archer uses his noggin' every now and then? I'm hurt," he said.

"While that was an amazing 'up yours' to my 'if, and, or but' scenario, it doesn't change the fact that we still have much to plan. Now let's go. I'll let you drink *one* shot." Mr. Yorke laughed, dragging Archer to the door.

"Goodbye, bullies." Archer saluted as the door closed.

Hazel slinked over to her mother, leaning into her legs as the commotion died down.

"Mama, I'm tired."

Sienna stooped down and picked Hazel up, resting the girl on her hip.

"Well, I think that's our cue to head out. We had a lot of fun today, Lukas, and I hope you enjoyed yourself, too," Sienna said softly. She dragged Lukas and Owen into a quick hug. "We'll see you all at the fair."

Lukas grinned. "Absolutely."

"We're going too, guys," Sawyer said. "Thanks for inviting us today."

"I need a twelve-hour nap," Eliseo groaned as he walked to the front door, stretching and yawning. "Glad you're the one driving, bruh."

"Me too because the way you drive is terrifying," Sawyer stated bluntly. "You drive like you're a star in *Driveby Delinquent*."

"Hey, it's a great game," Eliseo huffed as he leaned against the doorway. "Anyway, thanks for the invite, Luuu. We'll see you at the Hullabaloo."

The door shut with a final click. As the sound of Sawyer's car speeding off down the road died out, Lukas sighed, leaning against the door.

"Sweet, sweet silence. I don't know about you, but I'm ready to–"

Owen's feverish body was already against his, trapping him against the door in a tight embrace.

"Well, this wasn't my original plan, but I can get behind this," Lukas whispered, smiling.

"And coming up next, Kinetic Flaw with their new song, 'Why, Monkeys, Why?'"

Cheers erupted from the small crowd gathered in front of the jumbled stage. Archer jounced around it with his band members, who were poking fun at each other before they began their song.

Archer's band might not have been well-known outside of Boston, but the locals knew every release. The man had a habit of coming up with new tunes and songs while in the kitchen, and the customers loved every second of it.

Lukas clapped lightly from the booth, enjoying the shade more and more as the temperature rose. As the song started, he stared up at the clear, blue sky, feeling nostalgic. The Heated Hullabaloo was set up on a fairground north of Salem, far from the tall buildings of the center of Boston. Still not exactly like home, but close.

Despite the crowds already filling the fairgrounds, there were plenty of opportunities to take a breather and enjoy the atmosphere, especially with Mr. Yorke at his side.

"Rest for a while, Lukas. After that rush, it should

so slow down for a while." Mr. Yorke rearranged the dishes on the counter. "Or, not, as it would seem."

Lukas raised his head and saw Hazel rushing toward the booth, dragging Sienna behind her. She ducked under the plastic flap on the side of the tent and grabbed Lukas' arm.

"Lukas, come on! Eliseo has his shop set up! Let's go look at the pretty clothes!"

He looked over at Sienna, who shook her head with a smile.

"Nuh-uh. Don't look at me. Mama needs a break. She's been running like mad since the gates opened. Anyway, she wanted to show you a costume she liked."

"I suppose it can be arranged." Lukas stretched, sighing as his body relaxed. He let her take his hand and lead him deeper into the fairgrounds.

Lukas could instantly tell which tent belonged to Eliseo. Each wall was adorned with sketches of his past designs and different fabrics. The table he was frantically running around was covered with beautiful pieces of jewelry, each stone glittering brightly in the afternoon sun.

Lukas grinned as he got a good look at his friend. He was wearing a piece from his new steampunk collection. Not at all fitting for this event, but well-constructed and sensational. Atop Eliseo's shoulder sat his beloved bearded dragon, Newton Lysaurian Geckosli.

Hazel ran off, weaving her way through the crowd gathered around his booth. Sneaking under the tables, she poked up beside him, eliciting a fake scream from the man.

"Ha, I got you!" Hazel beamed.

Eliseo smiled coyly. "You may have gotten me, but Newton is the true threat!"

Eliseo snaked his arm down to Hazel's shoulder, letting the reptile scurry down to her. The girl giggled as the lizard ran along her arm.

"So, where's Sawyer? I thought he was supposed to be here with you," Lukas said.

"He'll be coming in about an hour. He got a last-minute order at his shop that needed to be taken care of before he could close it down," Eliseo said.

"There are a lot of new designs here. New muse?" Lukas asked.

"Been experimenting. Found the most beautiful piece at that antique shop I was telling you about. Victorian, 1839. Goes great with my steampunk collection."

"You sure that's all?"

Lukas was referring to the glances directed toward a young man running maintenance on the nearby rides that hadn't opened yet. "You keep sneaking glances at Abraham."

"You know him?" Eliseo gasped.

"Of course. He comes to the diner all the time." Lukas picked up a small ring, idly turning it over. The reflected, red hues from the gem danced across his face. "So, when are you gonna go talk to him? You are gonna talk to him, right?"

"Well, I mean… maybe. Maybe not. Just look at him. He works hard and doesn't talk much, but look at him. I know he's a beta, but I've had my eyes on him for a while. I just feel drawn to him. From those smoldering eyes to those tight coveralls. He's covered in sweat, but I wouldn't mind working up a sweat with–"

"Psst!" Lukas motioned to Hazel, who was still standing nearby, playing with Newton.

"Relax. Who said I was talking about–"

"Psst!" Lukas covered Eliseo's mouth with his

hand, causing his friend to snicker. "You forget, I've known you for years. I know your true thoughts."

"Well, it looks like you're about to have more to worry about than my foul mouth," Eliseo said.

"What do you—"

"Baaaaaabe!"

Lukas was grabbed by a strong arm and pulled back against a broad chest. A strong scent of sunscreen hit his senses, causing his nose to crinkle.

"You have got to try this." Owen waved a piece of chocolate-covered cheesecake on a stick in front of his face.

His free arm wrapped around Lukas' waist.

"Oi, get a room, you two." Eliseo stuck his tongue out at the pair and glanced over at Abraham.

"How about a table?" Sienna's voice cut in.

"No!" everyone yelled, looking shocked that she would even suggest such a thing.

"Such indecency, Sienna," Lukas gasped.

"I mean to sit at, fools! Archer was looking for everyone."

"Tell him to look harder. I can see his mangy golden mane from here just fine," Eliseo quipped, turning to answer a question from someone who was looking at his jewelry.

"Whatever. Just get over to the table as quickly as possible." Sienna took Hazel by the hand and led her back to the table.

"Wonder what he wants? He's been running himself ragged between the booth and the stage."

Lukas turned and saw Owen attempting to hide a smile.

"You know something." Lukas' eyes narrowed.

"I don't know what you're talking about." Owen crossed his hand over his heart.

"What sort of mess are we about to be thrown into?" Lukas asked.

Owen simply smiled as he wrapped an arm around Lukas' shoulders and led him back to the table.

A million thoughts were racing through Lukas' head. The baby shower was already done and over with, his birthday wasn't until October, and wasn't Archer supposed to be on stage?

"Oh, Christ. This is it," Lukas whispered.

"What?"

"You've all spent time getting close to me, and now my time has come. This is going to be a modern-day *Clue* game. 'Who killed Lukas?'"

"You've been watching too many crime shows. I liked it better when you watched the cooking channel nonstop. It makes you all happy and dancy." Owen laughed.

As they approached the table, the conversation died down, which didn't do anything to help Lukas' unease.

"Okay, so what's everyone being so secretive for?" Lukas asked.

Archer stood from the table. "Come one, come all! Watch as I, Archer Moodnifico, grant your wildest desires!"

"You're a fairy godmother!" Hazel squealed.

Archer visibly shrank back as if the little girl had assaulted him.

"No, no. I am–!" Archer started before sighing. "Nah, forget it. Yes! I am a fairy godmother. Now, you see, a little birdie tweeted in my ear about a recent arrival to Boston. Please, give him a warm welcome."

Lukas froze as Colton stepped out from behind the old oak tree their table sat under.

"Hey, little brother." Colton's voice was small and quiet, unfitting for an alpha. Worry twinged his few words.

The world seemed to come to a standstill as both brothers were speechless. A slow grin formed on Lukas' face as tears welled up in his eyes.

"Well, that little birdie didn't sing no song for me!" Lukas laughed as he pulled his brother into a hug.

Colton seemed shocked by the younger man holding him in an iron grip before he slowly wrapped his arms around his brother.

"Has it really been that long?" Colton asked.

"Too long. Way too long," Lukas sniffled.

Colton carefully pulled back, taking a piece of paper out of his shirt pocket in a hurry. "Whoah, don't cry! The other part of the surprise will be ruined!"

Lukas tensed up. "Oh, ya'll are killin' me here. It's not even close to my birthday yet."

Colton gave the small piece of paper to Lukas.

Lukas cautiously took it and stared at it for a moment. "Well, it's not a pink slip, so I know Sienna didn't conspire to get me fired."

"I would never."

"Now, where have I heard that before?" Owen whispered.

Sienna glared at the alpha. "Hush, you. Read it, Lukas."

Carefully unfolding the paper, Lukas began to read aloud.

"To Lukas McGuire, in appreciation for your acts and services to the city of... *The Roaring Ridgemont Eatery?*"

Archer spoke up, "I wanted it to sound official. Keep going."

"We would like to present you with the… *behind curtain number one: it's a brand new co-ownership of The Roaring Ridgemont Eatery!?*

Lukas snickered. The writing was so bad and really did not fit on the line provided. Then, it hit him.

"Wait, seriously?"

"You gotta read the best part!" Hazel squealed.

"Owning a part of the diner isn't the best part?" Lukas asked.

Hazel pointed to the bottom of the paper. "No. Read the rest."

Lukas took a deep breath before continuing, "Formally signed by *Bitty-Piggy, the Bacon Bit of Porkington…* Bitty-Piggy?"

Colton spoke up, "Bitty-Piggy is my pet. She's a micropig. I told Archer her name, but he thought a micropig should be named Bacon Bit, so we compromised."

"And she's so cute." Hazel beamed.

Colton smiled. "The cutest."

"So, what say you, Lukas? Do you accept the micropiggy's gift?" Archer asked.

"Absolutely. I will work hard and bear the whisk in her name."

"And so it shall be!" Archer announced.

Dusk settled over the fairgrounds as the rides and booths began to glow, the lights reflecting gaudy shades of pink, yellow, and green across the ground.

"We're gonna have to find a supplier," Lukas idly said. "I don't think I'll be able to keep up with just a small garden of berries."

"Just promise me one thing: no back-alley

suppliers. You're classier than that, babe," Owen joked as he munched on a piece of funnel cake.

"Find me a reputable supplier of blueberry cocaine, then we'll be in business." Lukas laughed.

"That's one way to make your goods stand out," Owen said.

A peaceful moment drifted by. Lukas' stomach rumbled as the smell of fried foods drifted down the gravel pathways. Songs blasted from the stage as people huddled around the best rides and booths. Costumed performers strolled between the fairgoers, wresting jeers and laughter from the crowds.

Lukas sighed contentedly, "Almost reminds me of the county fairs back home. Only one thing missing."

Owen perked up, draping his arm across Lukas' shoulders. "What's that?"

"The stars. That's one of the things I like about being outside this time of year. Back home, there was always a cool breeze flowing through the valley. Evening would come and paint the sky with the touch of an artist. So many beautiful colors. Then, the stars would come out, sparkling like diamonds." Lukas stared up at the darkening sky.

Owen was quiet for a moment before pulling out his phone and sending a few text messages. It wasn't long before he was pulling Lukas to his feet.

"Come on. They can spare us for a few minutes," Owen whispered.

"What's up?" Lukas questioned.

Owen smiled and led him to the parking lot. "You'll see. I have a plan."

The sounds and lights of the fairgrounds died out behind them as they pulled onto the road, heading down what Lukas guessed would be a backroad by Boston's standards.

A quiet song on the radio filled the silence. Lukas

leaned his seat back a bit and folded his hands behind his head, staring at the passing silhouettes of the trees against the pink and purple sunset.

Lukas closed his eyes for a few minutes before he heard the crunch of gravel beneath the car.

"We're here, sleeping beauty." Owen came around to open the door for Lukas. "Come on."

Owen led Lukas down a covered path to a clearing overlooking the distant fairgrounds. He could still hear the lighthearted fair music.

"Hold up. I've seen this movie before," Lukas quipped.

"But I bet you haven't seen a view like this." Owen raised his head to look at the dark sky. "At the very least, not in a long while."

Lukas followed his gaze. His mouth dropped open when he saw the painted sky covered in twinkling lights.

"Starry skies for my omega," Owen whispered, taking Lukas' hand.

"You're gonna make me cry again," Lukas whimpered.

"If you cry, you won't be able to see what's next."

Feeling Owen's gaze on his back, Lukas turned around. Owen's fiery eyes were full of such raw emotion, he felt himself become hot and bashful under their intense stare.

"Christ. You know, I never thought I'd be in this position. Just a couple months ago, I was in a crappy apartment in Las Vegas, pouring drinks for the high and mighty. Now, I live with you and the critters, and in a few months, our baby will be here. I feel like I have it all. All except one thing."

Owen crouched on one knee and reached for his back pocket.

"Oh, God. Is this really happening?" Lukas thought to himself.

"So, I have only one question for you. Will you marry me?"

This was it. This was his own version of an out-of-body experience. He could pretty much see himself standing there like an idiot as Owen proposed to him. Except he wasn't dead. At least, he hoped not. Was this actually happening?

Owen's concerned voice reached his ears, "Babe? Did I break you?"

"I think my heart just melted," Lukas whispered. "Yes, yes, yes, you big dork. Of course, I'll marry you."

Lukas launched himself onto his alpha, tears flowing freely as he peppered kisses all over Owen's face. Owen laughed as he wrapped his arms around his omega.

"You know, I'll be honest. I had a much more passionate proposal speech planned out in my head before we came up here," Owen said.

"What do you mean? I'm not marrying the speech, I'm marrying the man, and I know how passionate the man is, no matter how his words are spoken," Lukas gasped.

"It turned out a lot better than I thought it would, but I forgot most of what I had planned to say when you turned around, and I saw your face. You were just…it was a perfect moment. The lights of the fair and sky behind you—you were almost glowing."

"I still would have said yes, even if you had only managed to get out a few words," Lukas snickered, sidling up to his alpha.

Owen laughed. "It would have been like 'You marry? Please do. Me love.'"

"Like I said, I'm marrying the man, not the

speech." Lukas grinned. "This really was perfect, though. Now comes the fun of planning."

Owen spoke up, "Hazel can be the flower girl."

"And Sawyer can do the flower arrangements," Lukas said.

"As long as I get to be the maid of honor." Archer's gruff voice came from the nearby grove.

Lukas jumped, staring at the grove they had come from. Owen simply grinned, turning back toward the sound.

Archer, Sienna, Eliseo, and Colton clamored into the open, Eliseo holding a small camera.

Colton stepped forward and gathered his brother and new brother-in-law in a bear-hug. "You're stuck with him now, Owen, bless your heart."

"I take offense to that, *brother.*"

"And that sounds like a personal problem, *baby brother.*" Colton grinned.

Lukas smirked. "Speaking of baby, tell me, how do you like the sound of Uncle Colton?"

Colton froze, stepping back in shock. "No way. Are you really…?"

"A few weeks along. Due around January or February." Lukas felt Owen take his hand in his.

"He accidentally announced it at Hazel's party." Sienna took the camera from Archer and put it in her purse.

"Oh? How do you accidentally announce something like that?" Colton asked.

"He got sick. And he never gets sick," Sienna snickered.

"Oh, man, I'm gonna be the uncle-iest uncle that ever– Bitty-Piggy!?"

Colton's sudden shout startled everyone as a small, squealing creature rushed into the clearing.

"She got away, catch her!" Sawyer yelled, arms

outstretched. Hazel followed him, struggling to keep up.

Bitty-Piggy ran straight to Colton and hid behind his legs. Colton easily scooped up the tiny pig with one hand.

Sawyer was so focused on catching the little pig, that when she was suddenly scooped up, he had to put on the brakes.

"Watch ou–!" Sawyer cut himself off as he began to slide forward, trying to slow himself.

Sawyer suddenly felt himself come to a stop. Colton had caught him in his other arm easily, and he unintentionally pulled the omega against his chest. Sawyer's hands were wedged between his own body and Colton's, resting on the alpha's chest.

The air suddenly grew tense as time marched on. Sawyer carefully wiggled his way out of a shocked Colton's embrace, apologizing profusely before heading back to the cars, red as could be.

Colton's shoulders drooped as Sawyer ran down the shrouded path.

"I don't think I've ever seen Sawyer get flustered like that," Lukas whispered to Eliseo.

"Same here. Did you feel that spark, though? Yowza," Eliseo whispered, looking back at Colton. Owen was already next to him, smirking.

"Colton? Colton, you okay?" Owen waved his hand in front of the other alpha's face.

Colton snapped out of it, stuttering, "I hope this doesn't sound creepy, but I think I know what angels smell like now."

"Do share this info, I'm curious." Eliseo laughed.

"Peonies, tea, and cinnamon? It's all… I don't know. What's the word I'm looking for?"

"Comforting, but at the same time, distracting?" Lukas offered.

Colton nodded, "Yes, exactly!"

Lukas smiled, saying, "That's how I knew Owen before I even met him. Archer would go to the bar when we started to plan the fair and bring back that scent, and I was always distracted but intrigued by it."

Colton sighed. "But fate is cruel."

"What are you going on about?" Lukas asked.

"I live down in Atlanta now, and long-distance, well, if he chose to… Not that I'm the only option, but…"

"Spit it out, brother!" Lukas said firmly. Colton jumped at his brother's raised voice.

"Long-distance usually ends up hurting both parties. I don't think I can do it. I want to be near my partner. I want to enjoy their presence, bask in their glow, take care of them as an alpha should. If not, I feel like they might just get…ripped away from me."

Archer spoke up, "So, just move up here."

"You make it sound so easy." Colton sighed.

"Come on, if I can do it, you can." Lukas smiled.

Owen nodded. "You know, if you do decide to come up here, you're always welcome to crash with us."

"What?" Colton looked wary, like someone was playing a prank on him.

"Yeah, I'm invading Lukas' space now." Owen grinned.

Colton's gaze drifted to the ground as Bitty-Piggy squirmed in his hands. "Maybe, but there's still the fact that I need a job to survive. I'm working as a biologist down in Atlanta."

"And there are tons of companies hiring here. I'm sure you could find a job easily," Sienna said.

Colton sighed. "I'll look into it. Definitely." He took a deep breath as he held Bitty-Piggy closer to his body. The shrouded path was empty and quiet now, and only a lingering scent of Sawyer remained.

"That spark was intense, though. I'm gonna have to pry some info from Sawyer about that because that was just... wow." Eliseo grinned. "You should try to talk to him again before you leave. Maybe he'll have calmed down by then."

Lukas smiled. "And that goes for you too, Eliseo."

"I don't know you." Eliseo crossed his arms and stuck out his tongue. "But I do have to get back to my booth. We closed it up before we came up here, and there's a ton of stuff I want to try to sell before I head home."

Eliseo began to walk down the path toward the cars, "And I suppose I should check on Sawyer, too. Did you see how red he was? Poor guy probably has a raging fever now," He snickered as he disappeared into the grove.

"Hang on!" Colton took long strides, trying to catch up with Eliseo before he turned around to talk to the group one last time. "I'll see you all back down at the fairgrounds!"

Archer laughed as he watched Colton rush down the path. Hazel had covertly followed him, hoping to spend more time with Bitty-Piggy.

"What a rush. I remember when I used to chase after my flames like that."

"Why'd you stop chasing?" Lukas asked.

"I got old." Archer laughed. "But seriously, I just grew up, I guess. While we may be tied together by the alpha, beta, and omega inside us, we're still human. I took relationships for granted when I was young and hurt many a beta and omega. Not physically, of course, just... I wasn't mentally prepared for commitment, and I can honestly say I was an idiot."

"You never know what lies around the corner, man. I mean, I told Lukas earlier that I was in a crappy apartment in Las Vegas just a few months ago. A single man with a single dog surrounded by strangers in a strange place. And now? Engaged with a baby on the way. Don't give up," Owen said. He hugged Lukas from behind, resting his chin on top of the omega's head.

"Bah, you two are young. Don't waste time worrying about me. I'm perfectly happy with my diner and the company of friends." Archer cocked his head and smiled. "But anyway, I'm gonna head back down, too. Sheldon is probably lonely without me."

"I don't think you have to worry about that, Archer. Sheldon is probably surrounded by his patrons. He always has an escort, it seems." Sienna smiled as Hazel came running back down the path with Bitty-Piggy in her arms. "I think we're gonna go ride the rides and eat all the food now. Congratulations to both of you. Keep us updated, okay?"

"Of course. Now, go have fun, Hazel. The fair is only around for a few days, after all!" Lukas reached out to pet Bitty-Piggy. "We'll be back down soon."

Hazel laughed as Bitty-Piggy squealed. She turned to Owen. "You'll have to ride the rollercoaster with me when you get back. Mama and Lukas don't like to ride them."

"I can do that, little princess. I will ride all the rides with you." Owen grinned.

Sienna and Hazel waved as they walked back down the path, leaving the pair alone under the stars.

"Engaged with a baby on the way. What a trip," Lukas murmured.

"A good trip. I can't wait to meet them," Owen

whispered, gazing down at Lukas with smoldering eyes.

Lukas sat down on the grass as he felt a cool breeze blow across his body. Owen followed, wrapping an arm around his fiancé and pulling him close.

"I love you, Lukas. I'm so happy that you're my everything," Owen breathed quietly.

Curling into the embrace, Lukas felt his body relax. "I love you, too."

Staring at the sky, Lukas felt at peace. What was once so empty was now brimming with life. He held his hand over his abdomen unconsciously. This was what love felt like. It was a comforting, full feeling, one that he was more than happy to share with his alpha now and forever.

"*I* don't understand. What's got you so riled up?" Lukas cocked his head, smirking.

"You're only in labor!" Owen practically trembled with anxiety.

Lukas thought for a moment, then replied nonchalantly, "This is true."

Owen paced the floor, wringing his hands, "How are you *not* riled up? Are you not in pain? Are you broken? Did I break you?"

"Babe, calm down. Take a deep breath," Lukas instructed. He gripped the edge of the bed, riding through a contraction, as he listened to Owen's panicked breaths.

"I'm the one who should be comforting you, not the other way around," Owen said. "How are you so zen right now?"

Lukas simply smiled and leaned back into the mattress.

"What's to worry about? Omegas are made to handle this. Remember? We did our research, we talked to the doctors. We know what's going to happen, what I'm going to feel, and what comes afterward."

"So what you're saying is that we're the baby-meisters?" Owen cracked a smile.

Lukas chuckled. "Hell no. Unless I'm suddenly a printer and they pull an instruction manual out with her, we're winging thi–"

Lukas' voice caught in his throat as another contraction rushed through his body.

Owen grasped Lukas' hand, watching the pained expression on his mate's face. "Oh, God. What's going on? Do I need to call the doctor?"

"It's nothing, don't worry. I'm just communing with Purrgak-ron."

"Forget the Old Gods, babe! This is–"

"Absolutely natural. Don't worry," Lukas interrupted Owen with a forced smile. *God, this really hurts.*

Owen started again, "But–"

"Calm."

Taking a deep breath, Owen rested his head on the uncomfortable plastic rail of the bed. "Okay. Okay, being calm. I am being one hundred percent chill."

The steady beep of the monitors echoed through the room as they rested. The calm before the storm, as it would seem.

Lukas leaned back, listening to the distant sound of sirens and traffic. The TV, turned down low, broadcasted the next week's weather forecast. It was a pleasant hum that distracted him momentarily from the pain in his abdomen.

Only momentarily.

Lukas cringed as another wave of pain pierced his body just as the doctor returned, the crisp white lab coat seeming overly bright in the florescent lights.

"How are we feeling in here? Is the little princess

about ready to make an entrance?" The doctor smiled, glancing between Owen and Lukas.

"You're the coachman, doc. The one bringing her to the ball, so to speak. What say you?" Lukas said hoarsely, riding out the last edge of pain.

"We're just about ready, my friends. I know you're excited to meet your girl. Don't worry, it won't be much longer. I'm bringing the team in now." The man grinned, scribbling on his clipboard as he stepped back toward the door. "Now's the time to call everyone if you want to plan a meet-and-greet in the next couple of days."

Lukas sighed as the door clicked shut. This was it.

"Can you let everyone know? I'm sure they're waiting on the edge of their seats," Lukas whispered.

"Can do, babe," Owen replied and called the crew.

Closing his eyes, Lukas relaxed into the lumpy pillow propped up behind him. A distant page for persons unknown echoed down the hallways of the hospital.

"Colton should be arriving sometime tomorrow," Owen said. "He said he's booking the next flight to Boston."

Owen plopped down in the chair next to the bed. "You know, I'm glad your brother thinks ahead. I mean, he told me he already settled things with the house, got all his furniture ready to go, and had a bag packed just in case our little Abi decided to make an early appearance. Can you believe that?"

"Well, he had to be the responsible one. It's like second nature to him," Lukas whispered. "I'm so happy he made the decision to move here."

Owen grinned. "I know. I'm gonna have so much fun harassing him."

"And Sawyer."

"What*ever* do you mean?" Owen feigned innocence.

Lukas chuckled. "You know I'm all for it. Did you see the way they looked at each other before Sawyer got all flustered? This needs to happen."

"We need to get Eliseo a person, too." Owen leaned forward, balancing his elbows on his knees.

"Yeah, you're right. But one thing at a time–"

Lukas doubled over as one last bolt of pain shot down his spine.

"Sweet Jesus, are my muscles disintegrating?" Lukas groaned, hearing angels sing as the door slowly opened again, revealing the doctor and his team.

"Alright, are we ready to get this show on the road?" The man asked, smiling warmly.

"We sure are." Lukas nodded, squeezing Owen's hand.

"We've been ready ever since we first knew her, doc," Owen whispered, bringing Lukas' hand up to softly kiss it. "Look out world, here comes another Atkins."

Lukas laughed, "God help us all."

EXCERPT

Book 2 Excerpt:
Forget Me Not, My Dear Omega

Colton's chest ached. He couldn't help but notice the way Sawyer's eyes softened as he spruced up the bouquet, talking more about the different meanings hidden within the flowers.

Eureka.

Colton perked up. That was it! Just like how he had conveyed a message to Sawyer with the need for Begonias, he could put together a letter in the form of flowers. Yes, flowers were more than just decorations, they could also be declarations. The language they spoke was universal, almost like music for the eyes!

Owen suddenly appeared beside him, snapping him back to reality.

"So what does Begonia mean? Is that some code word?"

Colton led Owen away from the counter, ready to get some fresh air. "It means 'beware' in the old Victorian flower language."

The two alphas stepped from the shop. Colton

looked back over his shoulder, feeling his chest tighten when he saw Sawyer glancing back.

He buried his face in his hand, thankful for the cold air outside.

I'm done for.

"I've made a decision," Colton whispered as the door shut behind them.

"You'll try the escamoles this time?" Owen gave a lopsided grin.

"Ew, no. No, I've decided that after my interview, I'm just gonna go for it. I need to tell him how I feel."

Owen paused before sitting down on a nearby bench, motioning for Colton to sit next to him.

"Tell me why," Owen gave him a side-glance, a neutral look on his face. "Tell me. This is an important step for you."

Owen's piercing eyes were something he never thought he'd be the victim of. Colton thought for a moment, glancing at his brother-in-law.

"There's just so much that happens whenever I'm around him... Where do I even begin?"

"Like you're reading a book, just start from the top. Don't think, just feel," Owen said, relaxing into the bench.

Colton leaned back on the bench, taking a deep breath before the words came tumbling out all at once.

"When I'm near him, I feel stronger, I feel like I have a purpose again. My heart races whenever I catch a scent of him, but, at the same time, I feel at peace. The world seems to move a bit slower when I see him, but I feel like the moment is over too fast when he smiles, when he laughs, or when he looks at me with those soft brown eyes."

Colton paused.

"I just want to learn all about him. I want to know

what he loves, every emotion, every face, every word, and every dream."

Breathing deeply, Colton puffed out his chest, confident gaze turning to Owen, "I want to be the one to protect him. He deserves safety and security. I swear, if he so chooses, I will do everything in my power to give him a happy life."

"Careful, your plumage is showing, bro." Owen raised his eyebrow.

"Don't you be sassin' my plumage."

Owen laughed, "And there you have it. You're all grown up! Way to go, man. So, what's your plan?"

Colton simply smiled, gazing up at the painted sky and skyscrapers.

"I'll make sure he remembers me."